THE WEEPING CHAMBER

Other Books by Sigmund Brouwer

The Carpenter's Cloth

Blood Ties

Double Helix

Magnus

The Ghost Rider Western Mysteries:

Morning Star

Moon Basket

Sun Dance

Thunder Voice

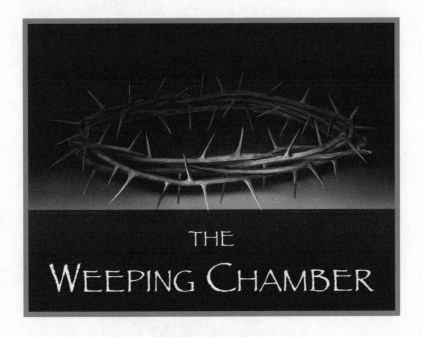

THE
WEEPING CHAMBER

Sigmund Brouwer

WORD PUBLISHING
Nashville•London•Vancouver•Melbourne

THE WEEPING CHAMBER

Unless otherwise indicated, Scripture quotations used in this book
are from The Holy Bible, New Century Version, copyright © 1987,
1988, 1991 by Word Publishing, Nashville, TN 37214.

Library of Congress Cataloging-in-Publication Data

Brouwer, Sigmund, 1959–
The weeping chamber : a novel / Sigmund Brouwer.
p.   cm.
ISBN 0-8499-3703-5
I. Title
PS3552.R6825W44   1998
813'.54—dc21
98-11033
CIP

Printed in the United States of America
8 9 0 1 2 3 4 5 9 QBP 9 8 7 6 5 4 3 2 1

*To Kip Jordon
We miss you.*

Preface

I cannot pretend to be a historian. In writing this book, I could only do my best as a novelist to reshape and bring to life what I learned from great writers and historians. I owe them much for enabling me to see these events with new eyes. I especially recommend time with Alfred Edersheim as he shares passionate history and deep faith in his book, *The Life and Times of Jesus the Messiah*.

Because I came to this book as a novelist, I hope readers will indulge my decisions to fix a specific time or place or character to some of the gospel events. My intent was to remain true to Scripture and to historical facts; I ask forgiveness should my efforts appear to fail in this regard.

I would like to thank Janet Reed, Laura Kendall, and Joey Paul for sharp eyes and excellent editorial intuition. I would also like to thank Reverend John Woods; as tour guide at the Garden Tomb in Jerusalem, his observations gave me the title of this novel and helped me understand what it would have been like to stand in the weeping chamber on that Sunday of hope.

Most of all, I am deeply grateful to my wife, Cindy. During my time with this novel, she was in the process of writing the music and lyrics to *The Loving Kind*, an album that explores these same days of Jesus' journey to the cross and beyond. That she and I were able to share time in Jerusalem as preparation for the novel was a joy; that she encouraged me as she did was a gift; that I was able to listen to her songs was joyous inspiration.

Prologue

I stand in the weeping chamber of my own tomb. I hear the dry wheezing of my old lungs. As I lean upon a cane for balance, my body shakes and trembles.

Behind me, the mouth of the tomb opens to the sunlight beyond. Despite the day's heat, here in the peculiar silence that fills any resting place for the dead, it is still cool. My cloak does not keep me warm, but I have given up on expecting my frail bones to hold any heat.

I stand in the weeping chamber of my own tomb.

It is not a large tomb. I purchased the rocky hillside decades ago and immediately hired stone workers to carve a narrow arched entrance the height of a man's head. Through this opening, the workers continued to hew into the hill, widening and clearing a space inside. When they finished, the tomb was as high as a man could reach and no more than seven steps in length or width.

They had measured me and chiseled into the rock inside the tomb a grave that would accommodate my body upon my eventual death. Beside it, they chiseled another measured space for Jaala, my wife. As was customary, they left the remaining graves rough and unfinished, waiting for our children to grow before determining the size of their resting places. Thus, the stone workers left two finished empty graves in the tomb beside four unfinished—when the work began, Jaala and I had a son and a daughter and were hoping for more children.

I stand in the weeping chamber of my own tomb.

After my death, mourners will work in this small area overlooking the graves, washing and anointing my body with oil and perfumes, wrapping me in the grave clothes made of long strips of linen, packing those linens with fragrant spices to take away the smell of death, and binding my head with a linen napkin.

I do not fear the thought of my death. Not after seventy years on this earth.

Nor do I stand in the tomb's weeping chamber to contemplate how eternity will sweep past my still body, leaving me behind to add to the dust of previous generations.

I stand in the weeping chamber because it is my yearly ritual.

Five of the graves remain empty.

It is the sixth that draws me into the tomb.

The expensive linen there has long since fallen into tattered strips; the body's odor has long since become a dry mustiness; the bones have long since collapsed into a small, sad pile that clearly shows my son died as a young boy.

He was my firstborn son. And the first dead.

I have mourned his horrible death for nearly forty years. . . .

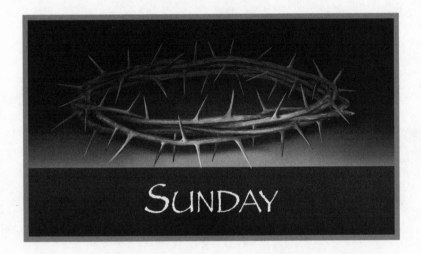

SUNDAY

1

My dearest love,

The servant who reads you these words will tell you that my hand is not steady. The prayer call of the priests' silver trumpets has yet to mark the dawn, and since I am unable to sleep, I write by the light of an oil lamp, knowing this activity will not disturb my hosts.

First, I wish you to know that I arrived safely for Passover, and I can report that Pascal and Seraphine are in good health. Now that my travel has ended, I have the luxury of applying markings to scroll. Far apart as we are, my intent is to begin each day of this week with you. I picture you listening to my letter and thus pretend we are in conversation. It aids me that I can imagine you reclining on your couch in our villa far above the harbor. I see your pretty head tilted sideways as you listen with your half-frown of concentration. The sun casts a shadow across your face, and the ocean breeze plucks at your soft dark hair much more gently than my rough fingers were ever able. It is how I like to dream of you.

Does it surprise you that I now take such trouble with words? Me? Your stony-faced husband who deals so harshly with sailors and merchants? I have not hired a poet as you might suspect. No, the distance between us makes my heart ache with sentiment, and it is easier to be weak for you when you cannot see how I tremble.

Last night, as I fell into troubled sleep, I could not escape thoughts of you: Your soft singing as you brush your hair. Your flashes of temper and immediate remorse. I remembered, too, our wedding, how you quivered with fear and anticipation and held me so tightly in our first moments alone that I thought my ribs would crack.

All I have are the thousands of memories with you since then. Simple memories. Watching you on the road from our balcony as you returned from the market with your arms laden. The perfume in your hair as we fell asleep together. The sight of you suckling our children. What we have lost in the present, I relive in the past.

Even on the road from Caesarea to Jerusalem, among the pilgrims on foot and riding wagons and mules, I found myself turning to you again and again in the crowd to share comments on the sights and sounds. You were not, of course, beside me, and on each occasion my heart grew heavier.

It is far worse, is it not, when you can only blame yourself for what is lost. When what you have lost becomes far sweeter because you will never have it again. Let us not fool ourselves. You no longer love me. That you are faithful, I have no doubt. But you do not love me.

I warn you now that in these letters I intend to pursue your hand with the same passion I did during our first days together. I want you to love me all over again.

Believing that you will mourn me is the only gift that gives me solace.

Yet when I find the courage to tell you what I must, I wonder how you could ever offer that gift. At the least, you will finally understand what has driven us apart. And why we will never be together again.

Until I find that courage, permit me these daily contemplations. Above all, think of my love for you.

2

Incense and silk. Scent and satin. Irresistible, at least to those who could afford it.

Absently—a touch once trained is a touch that would not forget—I ran my hand over a roll of dark silk in the front corner of the market shop. My fingers traced a few flaws, but I said nothing.

Three women stood in front of me, their veiled heads bobbing as they simultaneously haggled prices with my cousin Pascal.

I watched with as much amusement as I allowed myself in those days. The women had my sympathy. Their nostrils were filled with perfume, their grasping fists filled with draped silk and their husbands' purses of gold coins. Against Pascal's shrewdness, they stood little chance.

I waited patiently, knowing Pascal would allow them the small victory of an extended battle.

Although it was past dawn, little sunlight reached Pascal's wares. The shading was deliberate. He did not want his colors to fade. As well, dimness added confusion to a shop cluttered with rolls of silk and purple cloth, giving the impression that Pascal's luxuries spilled endlessly and sloppily, waiting for a buyer to take advantage of his carelessness. While the first was true—Pascal did have wealth a king might envy—not a single thread of silk floated out the door without Pascal's knowledge and consent.

When the women happily admitted defeat and walked past me with their armloads of wares, I turned so they could not see the angry burn scar that showed through my beard on the left side of my face. Their veils hid their eyes, but not their sight.

"Did you sleep well?" Pascal asked.

In the middle of his forties, he was fifteen years older than I. The night before, when I had arrived at his mansion in the upper city, I had seen him for the first time with his new wife. They made an interesting contrast. She, young and plump with golden-red hair, a ready smile, and plain clothing. He, old and thin and bald above a scraggly white beard, dressed in layers of luxury and chains of gold. Yet, I would not second-guess Pascal's choice of wives; he had already outlived three and could be expected by now to have decided what he did and did not like in a woman.

"I slept well," I said.

"That is a poor lie." He gave me his toothy lion's grin. "You do not look rested."

I shrugged.

Pascal pointed to where I had been standing. "That roll of silk you examined . . ."

"Adequate quality," I said, "but merely adequate, despite its rich appearance. I think water has marked it."

"Praise be to God that you do not choose to set up a shop opposite me here in Jerusalem." Another toothy grin. "You are right, of course. Fools and camels and a sudden rainstorm. I paid a fraction of what it is worth. As you might guess, however, I will not take that into consideration when the wives of rich men—"

"Pascal, purchase everything I have," I said bluntly.

My words stopped him flat, probably the first time I had seen him unable to immediately grasp a situation.

"My ships, my warehouses, my shops," I said. "Everything."

He recovered, his toothy grin replaced by serious study. He knew me well enough to understand I did not speak frivolously. He also knew me well enough not to ask for the reason behind my sudden offer.

"For a fair price, of course," he said, not so subtly testing me.

"Perhaps less," I answered. "I am far less concerned about the price than you might imagine."

He studied me, looking past my appearance.

"If it is not price, what, then, is your concern?" he finally asked.

"Honor," I said. "That is why I decided to use Passover as an excuse to come to Jerusalem and approach you."

Two women entered the shop. Pascal did not have the opportunity to ask more.

As for me, I was satisfied. I had planted the seed that would rapidly grow. By week's end, I guessed, Pascal and I would come to terms.

I left him with his customers and wandered out to see the city.

This was not my first visit to the Holy City. I knew what I would find as the markets came to life over the next few hours.

The streets would be crowded with bazaars, peopled with shoemakers, tailors, flax spinners, goldsmiths, wool combers, butchers, food inspectors, and diplomats. The air would be filled with the smell of fish, of incense, of ripe and rotting fruit, of the stench of leather being cured, tanned, and dyed. I would find food and wine shops, where, if my appetite conquered my dull spirit, I could partake from a selection that varied from fried locusts to fresh fish to fruit cakes. Or I could be tempted by Judean or Galilean wines, or a wide range of foreign beers to break my recent vow to avoid drink.

If I were after excitement, I could have dodged thieves and prostitutes in the lower city, among the dark underground alleys where a man could lose his soul and life to any number of different seductions. Or I could have cheered at the horse races in Herod's Hippodrome, or disappeared into a theater in pursuit of distraction, or lost myself in the hot fog of steam rooms that were as luxurious as any in Rome.

I knew, however, that no amount of activity would console me.

I chose instead to seek the countryside beyond the city, using as my guide the distant smoke of the temple sacrifices, which rippled dark above the altar like a curtain between earth and heaven.

3

I spent the remainder of the morning in the dusty groves above the Kidron Valley, on the western slope of the Mount of Olives. From there I could quietly survey all of Jerusalem. A few hours later, I returned to the main road and joined the pilgrims moving into the Holy City. I could not know then, of course, how I was about to become part of an inexorable movement about to destroy the single innocent man who stood resolutely in its path.

Not until later would I understand more, learning portions of it from those prominent in religious and political circles who welcomed me because of my wealth. Many of the other participants—servants and scribes, women and soldiers—later recounted their witness to his followers. When combined with what the followers themselves had seen, this entire story eventually became clear to me; I lean heavily on their record for what I was unable to see myself.

And what I could not see that morning began on the other side of the hill.

To be more accurate, the events began in Bethpage, which lay on the eastern side of the Mount of Olives. Some considered Bethpage distinct from Jerusalem, for the deep

Kidron Valley separated it from the city proper. Others—despite the valley between—considered Bethpage an extension of the city, and during Passover and the days before, the scattered collection of buildings that made up the hamlet were filled with festive pilgrims who could not find room to stay in Jerusalem.

Bethpage is connected to Jerusalem by a caravan road that crosses the bottom of the Kidron Valley and passes by olive groves as it climbs the Mount of Olives. After the road reaches the top, it dips through Bethpage, then continues on a gentle descent into Bethany, a half mile away. From there, the caravan road reaches to Jericho and beyond.

Little traffic, however, followed the road away from Jerusalem at this time of year. Instead, patriarch pilgrims jammed the road destined for the Holy City. Their bickering with mothers-in-law, camels, donkeys, chickens, children, and other stubborn beasts irritated by long days of travel provided amusement for the residents of Bethpage who sat beside their homes and watched the parade.

The crowds were at their most entertaining, for so near to Passover, people were impatient to reach the Holy City for purification in the temple. Furthermore, the warming weather had called out the idle who had already found lodging. The sky was weak blue in the high altitude, painted with wisps of clouds. A slight breeze kept the day from becoming hot, yet the sun had enough strength to banish all thoughts of winter.

Among the traffic, two men approaching Bethpage gave little cause for notice until they began to untie a young donkey haltered to a post near its mother before an inn.

Peter—red-headed and red-bearded—wore the rough clothing of a fisherman, with a sword strapped to his side and the perpetual scowl of suspicion common to laborers who understand no way to make money except with their hands. The other, John, taller with thinning brown hair, walked with a staff.

Fumbling with the rope at the donkey's side, Peter and John tried to ignore the hostile stares from a group of men nearby. The older men sat on chairs, surveying the road in dignified disdain; the younger men stood behind them with their arms crossed, trying to appear equally important to passersby.

"You!" the tallest of the younger men challenged, stepping toward them. "Red and stubby! Mind giving an explanation?"

Mutters of support came from the others.

Peter said nothing.

"You!" the man repeated. "Are you deaf? Touched in the head?"

Peter straightened, his hands still on the halter rope. "I can hear you with no difficulty. As for my head, there is nothing wrong—"

"Ho ho," the man laughed. He was bulky with the natural advantages of an athletic body, but his substantial belly showed he took his prowess for granted. "But a few words and I can tell you're from the north. All they grow are simpletons up there."

He paused, looking to his companions for support. Their grins were all the encouragement he needed.

"So tell me, country boy. What are you doing?"

The tendons at the side of Peter's neck strained as he tried to control his temper.

"This is a rope," Peter said slowly. "The rope is attached to the donkey. My fingers are upon the rope. As my fingers pull apart the knot, the rope becomes untied. Once I untie the rope, the animal will be free. It is a simple concept. Surely even the dimmest of minds can—"

"Peace, Peter," John interrupted him. "And remember our instructions."

John spoke directly to the gathered men, recalling how he had been instructed. "Our Lord needs this donkey. He will send it back shortly."

Peter's chest rose and fell visibly as he took in and let out a deep breath.

"Tell me," one of the older men said, speaking to John before a fight could erupt. "This Lord of yours. Would he happen to be the prophet from Nazareth?"

"None other," John replied.

The group's silence became a silence of respect.

"We have heard rumors of his arrival. Will he pass by soon?"

John nodded.

The old man thought for several seconds. "The story about a dead man, Lazarus of Bethany. Were you there?"

John nodded again.

"Was it as described?" the old man asked.

"Words do not do it justice," Peter said stoutly. "I smelled the stench of death from the tomb. And from the darkness he came, called out by our Lord."

The others whispered among themselves.

"Silence," the old man barked. To John and Peter he spoke more quietly. There could be no harm and possibly great gain in extending a favor to a famous worker of miracles. "Take the animal."

Both disciples led the donkey toward Bethany, where the teacher had already begun leading a procession on foot.

As soon as Peter and John turned a corner in the road, the young men before the inn scattered to spread the news in all directions, taking proud ownership in the arrival of the miracle man of Nazareth by being the first to have knowledge of his coming.

This news reached me as I walked among the pilgrims on my return to Jerusalem, news that stirred me from thoughts of despair and aroused a little curiosity from my depths of self-pity.

As for the old men, after the departure of the two disciples, they merely waited by the side of the road. They had long since learned that much of life arrived with or without their efforts.

4

With pilgrims surrounding the donkey, Yeshua rode in silence, cushioned from the vertebrae of the animal's spine by cloaks provided by his disciples.

Beside the animal, among the twelve of the teacher's closest followers, walked Lazarus, smiling and vigorous, the picture of anything but a man who some claimed had once been dead. Behind them, maintaining a respectful distance, were the women who took comfort from Yeshua's presence and teachings.

The small group of pilgrims traveling from Bethany—close followers and friends of the teacher—was also silent. Politically astute, the followers feared Jerusalem's reaction to his arrival. For some time, public postings had dictated that any person who saw the man from Galilee must report him. If he had chosen to arrive in full view and defiance of the temple authorities, however, they were not going to abandon him. Not yet.

The procession continued toward Bethpage. As the caravan road from Jericho left Bethany behind, it remained a broad, easily traveled mountain trail. The footing was rock, loose stones, and sand, paler brown than the reddish soil of the arid hills of Jericho. The Mount of Olives sloped upward on one side of the road and dropped steeply on the other.

Unexpectedly, as the travelers neared Bethpage, they saw a stream of pilgrims heading toward them, away from Jerusalem. These pilgrims were loud, almost boisterous in their enthusiasm.

Peter, walking a few paces behind the donkey, squinted as he tried to make sense of it. But too many hours of fishing with sunlight bouncing off the lake had made his sight notoriously untrustworthy among his friends.

"What's that?" he whispered to Judas. "A mob? Why?"

Judas Iscariot, a thin, handsome man with a well-trimmed beard, grinned. "Ask the teacher. He knows everything."

"He doesn't appear to be in the mood for jokes," Peter said. Judas had a knack for ill-timed humor. "Those people, what are they carrying?"

The red-headed fisherman's hand had unconsciously fallen to the hilt of his sword.

"Relax, hothead," Judas said. "Those are branches."

The larger crowd swept toward them. I was among that crowd. After hearing the babble and rumors and excitement and stories regarding this man, my curiosity had grown.

And so, I was about to see him. I had no idea how the intersection of our lives would change who I was.

"Is this the prophet from Nazareth in Galilee?" a man near me shouted.

"It is," one of the followers called back.

Shouts and cries carried back to reach those behind me. The crowd swelled forward. A few in the front removed their cloaks and placed them on the road.

Others began waving branches. And yet others shouted for Lazarus to step forward, to prove he was alive.

Somewhere from the middle of the throng came the first cries of praise.

"Hosanna! Blessed is he who comes in the name of the Lord! Hosanna!"

As I well knew from my previous Passovers in Jerusalem, people were shouting the welcoming chant from one of our ancient psalms—this was often extended to pilgrims. According to tradition, the pilgrims would respond with the second clause of each verse, with both parties singing the last verse together.

This occasion proved to be different from tradition, however. Much different.

Before us walked Lazarus, whose miraculous rising from the dead provided heated debate, speculation, and awe among the pilgrims to the Holy City. Lazarus was the proof, they cried, proof that all the other stories could be believed! Proof that a new Messiah had arrived to fulfill the ancient prophecies, a new Messiah with powers to break Roman oppression!

As a man of wealth and education, I did not need such stories to entertain me. Still, I understood how the stories could affect common people who had little variation or hope in their daily lives.

The crowd's fever grew, and the hosannas became hoarse, broken utterances. From voice to voice, from soul to soul, the fire of unencumbered joy spread.

"Hosanna! Blessed is the King of Israel! Blessed is the coming kingdom of our father David! Hosanna!"

Yeshua did not alter the pace of the donkey. People had plenty of time to rip down more branches to throw onto the road before the animal.

As the long procession spilled over the highest ridge to begin descending the Mount of Olives, the twelve followers finally saw the true extent of the crowd behind me and understood how the joyful noise could have reached such deafening levels.

The followers were dazed by the wonder of it all. This was no death march, they told themselves! This was a celebration of thousands streaming out through the gates of Jerusalem to join a spontaneous parade up the Mount of Olives. The majority were visitors to Jerusalem, most of them hardly aware of why they were dancing and singing with strangers.

This was no death march! Surely now the teacher did not have an execution to fear in Jerusalem. Not with the support of so many people.

"Hosanna! Hosanna! Blessed is the King of Israel! Blessed is the coming kingdom of our father David! Hosanna! Hosanna!"

The singing was so joyous, it almost lifted me from my despair. The singing remained joyous for some time—until a group of Pharisees pushed through the crowd.

These men were set apart by their religious caps and the tassels on their cloaks. Disgust showed obviously on their faces. Disgust at the possibility of contaminating themselves. Disgust at the spectacle of the public worship of a man they hated.

As the men began to shout and strike those around them, the hosannas quieted. Silence fell, all the more eerie in contrast to the almost frenzied shouting that had preceded it.

"Rebuke these people," the lead Pharisee commanded with the full authority of a man accustomed to making people shrink back simply by lifting an eyebrow. "You do not deserve this adulation. Call out now and send them away!"

The teacher slowly pulled his gaze from the view of Jerusalem. From where he sat, he could not see the temple or the northern portions of the Holy City. But to the south and east of Mount Zion, he could see rising terraces and the large homes of the wealthy Jews of the upper city. Yet the magnificent homes seemed dwarfed by the Palace of Herod, with its great towers and lush gardens. The white walls of the buildings glowed in direct sunlight, looking like the entrance to heaven.

The teacher stared at the Pharisees. He pointed at the rocks visible on the road, those not covered by the branches and cloaks spread before his donkey. Then he spoke slowly and clearly, so the crowd could hear his restrained anger. "I tell you, if my followers didn't say these things, then the stones would cry out."

The Messiah had spoken! New shouts of acclamation drowned out anything the Pharisees might have said in reply.

Unbidden, the donkey moved forward. The teacher swayed gently with its movement and ignored the Pharisees as he passed them.

The procession surged toward the final descent into Jerusalem.

5

A girl and a boy—scruffy, dirty children whose parents obviously had little concern for their whereabouts—dodged and twisted among us as we moved closer to Jerusalem.

The girl chased the boy past me, under the waving branches and palm leaves, both children unaware of the reason for celebration but giddy with laughter and the joyous mood of the adults around them.

They shrieked with play until the boy shot into a gap in the crowd. Although space opened for him, he stopped so quickly that the girl tumbled into him. She lifted her hand to slap the boy in mock vexation, but the sight that had mesmerized him stayed her hand, and she, too, froze to stare upward in awe.

A man on a donkey rode beneath the branches held aloft like a royal arch.

They saw what I had first seen.

The man's features were neither ugly enough nor handsome enough to set him apart from other men. His hair was neither shaggy nor cut in a fashionable style. His physique was compact from carpenter's work, but not overwhelming. This was a man easy to overlook on a crowded street. Except for his eyes.

Men and women looked into his eyes and felt eternity tug at their souls; a music of peace seemed to still time until finally, reluctantly, they were able to pull their eyes from his. These were eyes with the authority to cast aside demons of torment, eyes that with a single look could make a person whole. Eyes that made his smile unlike any other man's.

It had been this smile that had first riveted the boy. When the girl joined him, the man cast it upon her too. He focused his gentle attention on them with a gaze of such presence that a silence of instinctive untroubled yearning covered them like the cloaks upon his donkey, a silence so powerful that years later, in occasional quiet moments, this memory would soothe their souls as a caress.

I understood why the children stared. His eyes had kept me there in the crowd, unable to leave with a cynical snort of derision at the madness of the crowd's behavior; his eyes had cast the first doubts on my disbelief of the Lazarus miracle.

Then the moment ended for the boy and the girl.

The throng surged forward, moving the animal down the road. Pilgrims swept in front of the children, blocking their view of the man riding it.

In unison, without exchanging words or glances, the two turned, squeezing and bumping around the legs of the chanting adults in their need to follow. They stayed with us as the road dipped into a shallow depression. When the road rose again, it suddenly brought the Holy City into full view for the first time.

The temple tower dominated the line of the sky as easily as it lorded over the vast courts spread beneath it. And the monstrous temple walls were cliffs—unassailable and as fixed as eternity. The white lime paint of the buildings, the burnish of hammered gold on the temple, and the softness of the green of the gardens gave an impact of unearthly splendor, an ache of beauty that could never be captured by words.

What the children could not see, the man they followed did. Time's curtain rippled, shifting until it parted to give him a ghastly vision: of the same city with earthen ramps heaped to the top of the walls, of legions of soldiers swarming triumphantly, of the sky marred by the smoke of destruction, of temple walls shattered to rubble, of hills stark with hundreds of rebels impaled and groaning from crosses so numerous it was like a charred forest, of wailing mothers searching the ruins for their children's torn bodies. And then, with another ripple of the curtain of time, a new vision came: of dust swirling in an eerie dance to a haunting dirge sung by the wind as it blew across a plateau lifeless and desolate for centuries, the rejection by God as a horrible, cold punishment for a city that had butchered his son.

What the children could not see, the man on the donkey saw clearly: the beauty of the city and the inexorable tragedy ahead. The force of the contrast tore from him a wrenching sob so loud it startled those beside him. His sorrow deepened into heaving lamentation that cast the circled followers into an uneasy, puzzled silence.

It was as if he spoke to the women of the city when the agonized words left his mouth. "I wish you knew today what would bring you peace. But now it is hidden from you. The time is coming when your enemies will build a wall around you and will hold you in on all sides."

He closed his eyes but was unable to shut out the vision. "They will destroy you and all your people, and not one stone will be left on another. All this will happen because you did not recognize the time when God came to save you."

His weeping did not stop.

The boy and the girl crept forward. Unlike the adults, they were not frightened by the terrible sorrow of the man on the donkey but filled with a longing to comfort, as if he were a smaller child in need, and his sorrow drew them slowly to the donkey, where each shyly rested a hand on its flank.

For as long as he wept, they wordlessly shared his grief.

6

When the procession continued on toward Jerusalem, a conversation took place, one that I would learn of later from well-placed friends who enjoyed telling me of their successes. Friends, I am ashamed to say, accustomed to political intrigue.

If that says something about my character—to have such friends—I accept the judgment. It is part of the danger that comes with accumulating wealth, and there was a time in my life when I found it exciting to associate with such people—before I realized the price I was paying for my gold by giving it more devotion than I did my wife and children.

These friends I mention had sent spies to fish among the twelve followers of the man of Galilee. Later, they conveyed the conversation to me as follows. . . .

"Hello, my friend."

Walking behind the others, Judas glanced at the man who joined him. Older and of medium height, the most striking portion of the man's face was a bulbous nose, skin thick and pitted. The man's smile was ingratiating, dulled by several missing teeth.

"Who calls me friend?" Judas asked. He carried the moneybag for all the disciples. His natural shrewdness with money also made him naturally suspicious.

"Does it matter in this great crowd? We are all for the Messiah, are we not?"

Despite the ringing of song and cheers that had resumed around them, Judas caught the duplicity in the man's voice.

"We are," Judas said evenly.

"And you are one of his closest followers. Judas Iscariot. A Judean when all the others are Galilean."

That the man knew Judas's name was one thing. That he was prepared to show this knowledge was another. It was the essence of Judas to understand cunning subtlety. He knew the man was playing a game and was unafraid to show it. What game, however, roused Judas to curiosity.

"It is a great thing to be close to someone with such power, is it not?" the man continued.

Judas lifted an eyebrow, not agreeing, not disagreeing. At this point, it was in his interest to listen without committing any kind of answer.

"After all," the man said, "if he ever led crowds like this to a successful revolt, he would need capable administrators. Which, of course, is another sort of power."

The man alluded to the position Judas held among the disciples, showing he had even more knowledge about their workings. Outwardly, Judas hid his enjoyment of the intrigue.

They walked without speaking for a few steps. Halfway down the Mount of Olives now, they passed through the mottled shadows of olive trees.

"After all," the man said, content that he had Judas's interest, "if half of the stories of his miracles are true, with a single word he could fell Roman armies."

"They are true," Judas said. "My own eyes claim witness."

"Yes, yes," the man answered, still smiling his ingratiating toothless smile, "but in the region of Dalmanutha, a group of Pharisees challenged him to show a sign from heaven, and he was unable to produce a miracle. Had he but taken that opportunity . . ."

"My own eyes claim witness to his miracles," Judas repeated.

"Then why has he not taken the cloak of Messiah? I have spoken to other followers who left him. Followers who tell me that in Capernaum, he commanded them not to rise up against the Romans. Surely you saw how many fell away from him?"

Judas could not rise to his teacher's defense. For somehow, this grubby man had squeezed juice from the very same doubts Judas held.

"Yes," the man mused, "there is such a thing as a sinking ship. I, for one, would never hesitate to swim to safety. There is nothing noble about drowning unnecessarily, particularly if power is to be found elsewhere."

He winked at Judas. "You asked me my name, friend? Should you ever want to know, you may find me among the Sanhedrists. Those who hold true power."

He gave Judas a final oily smile before blending back into the flow of pilgrims.

7

"Simeon, you are quiet this evening." I brought my attention back from the flame of the oil lamp. Dusk had yet to arrive, and although the room received ample sunlight through the slatted window overlooking the central courtyard, Seraphine had insisted on the flame and incense to accompany the meal.

I found both Seraphine and Pascal staring at me. Pascal, I guessed, was curious because of our earlier conversation in his shop, a curiosity I did not wish to attend to immediately. Seraphine, perhaps, was still accustoming herself to the sight of a scarred cousin from a distant land, trying to match my appearance to all the wild stories Pascal had undoubtedly told about me before my arrival.

I attempted a wan smile at their concern. "Travel has left me weary."

"That was your excuse yesterday," Pascal said. He paused to swirl his wine, sniff it, and leave some on his tongue several seconds before swallowing. "You are beginning to sound like an old woman."

"Pascal . . ." Seraphine began in admonishing tones.

"Don't start on me, wife," Pascal told Seraphine. "He and I are cousins and business partners, and I also lay claim to the privilege of old friendship."

Pascal took another swallow, grimaced, and handed her his wine cup. "We have better. Find it."

"Only if the steward delivered more today," she said tartly. "And don't show off by treating me as chattel."

Pascal lifted his bearded face to stare at her directly. For a moment, I saw the iron that made Pascal the king of Jerusalem silk merchants. So, obviously, did Seraphine. She hesitated only briefly, took the wine cup, and left with a defiant swish of her dress.

"I'll pay for that later," Pascal said a few seconds later. His grin was crooked, showing large yellowed teeth. "A man's a fool if he thinks he rules his own home."

I thought of my home overlooking the sea and of my wife on the balcony as the wind blew her dark hair when she loosened it to dance freely. Regret must have crossed my face. When Pascal spoke again, his tone was much gentler.

"What is it, my friend?" he asked. He gestured at the table loaded with salted fish, sweet meats, fried locusts, grapes, figs, honey, and breads. Jugs of beer, wine, and water sat among the plates. It was a feast for many although there were only three of us. "You have eaten little and refused all my wine. And the unexpected offer to sell everything you own . . ."

"One matter is not related to the other," I said. "We shall find time this week to discuss business. As for my appetite, again blame travel. I am older now. I do not recover as quickly."

"A few weeks at sea exhausted you?" Pascal did a masterful job of pretending the business matter was not foremost in his mind. "With a stopover in Alexandria? And a few days of rest in Caesarea? Don't lie to me, Simeon. I sent Seraphine away to give us time alone here, as you seem to disappear during the day and retire early upon your return."

"It is nothing." If he was trying to give me the opportunity to talk about the fire, I had no desire to oblige him.

"A dozen times over the last twenty years, you have joined me here for Passover. Each of those dozen Passovers, I was hard-pressed at any meal to keep your wine cup full. And now? All you take is water and bread. Is that why you have become so gaunt?"

"In the last months, I have fasted," I acknowledged.

"You? A religious man?" Pascal laughed. "I thought you were far too practical for that. And your love of wine and beer was—"

"It no longer suits me!" I said, surprised at the vehemence of my voice.

Pascal closed his eyes in instant remorse. "Forgive me for prying."

"There is nothing to pry," I said, trying to keep the edge out of my tone.

A moment later, I sighed. "There is nothing to forgive. As you said, it is a privilege of old friendship to speak openly."

Pascal nodded as if he understood. But he didn't know my secret.

The day before, I had overheard him speaking to Seraphine: *Simeon has always been robust,* he'd told her, *with an air of dangerous wildness that attracted the wrong kind of women. Now, he is a different person. Where he once kept his thick dark hair long, it is nearly shorn and dull. And if that doesn't show something seriously wrong,* he'd added, *all you have to do is look at his skin, loose and parchment gray. Yes,* Pascal had concluded, *today's Simeon is not the Simeon of old.*

Seraphine's only response had been a cluck of sympathy. They both knew of the tragedy that had befallen my family. A son lost. A daughter crippled. And, of course, even if they had not received a letter from my wife Jaala, there was the scarred flesh of my face, mute testimony to the accident eighteen months earlier.

"Since we speak of religion," I said, looking to stop Pascal's speculations regarding my troubles, "tell me about this prophet from Nazareth. I was near the temple today, and he caused a tremendous stir."

Pascal poured himself some beer. He did not remark on the unusual aspect of my spending more than the required Passover time at the temple. *If he had gone as far as to fast*, I could read Pascal's mind, *where next would Simeon go? . . .*

"As you know," Pascal said, "a good many of my friends belong to the Sanhedrin. Caiaphas, the high priest, in fact, is one of my best customers. Of course, with the proceeds from temple sales, he can afford to be. Do you know what kind of profit there is in simply changing coins to the half shekels demanded for the yearly tribute? Let the peasants grumble if they will, but you have to admire the strong business sense of Annas and his family. They—"

"The prophet. The one they call the Messiah."

"We have had dozens of messiahs," Pascal snorted, unfazed by the directness of my question. "The countryside is rife with them."

"Dozens who raise men from the dead? Dozens who refuse to call for action against the Romans and instead preach love and compassion? Dozens who are followed by crowds of thousands?"

"You've heard the stories then. Understand that it is unsettling for those of us in Jerusalem."

"A dead person brought to life? Unsettling is an understatement. If it is true, then—"

"Truth has nothing to do with the situation," Pascal said. "This Yeshua could be a magician. Or he could be working with the devil, as some of the Pharisees say. Besides, what does truth matter against hard practicalities? This country is dry tinder, ready to be set ablaze by the tiniest spark. A so-called Messiah with a following is an open flame. Surely you, as a merchant, understand that."

"A revolt is bad for business," I said dryly.

"When business is good, life is good. Would you rather watch soldiers go through the city, killing men, women, and children? I've heard Caiaphas say it myself. Better that one should die than we all perish."

"So the prophet is marked for execution?" I asked.

"I'm surprised he marched publicly into Jerusalem. If you want to hear his teachings, you had better do it as soon as possible. If they can ever get him away from his adoring public . . ."

"Perhaps he is unafraid. If he can raise a man from the dead . . ."

Pascal dismissed me with a gulp of beer and a wave of his hand. "Don't give that rumor a second thought, my friend. Only God himself could do such a thing. And I doubt he would come from the backwaters of Galilee."

MONDAY

8

My dearest love,

Another day begins. It is so early that I again write by oil lamp, but soon, although the passage of time seems endless, the sun will rise.

I am tired. The night does not treat me well whether I sleep or not.

When I lie awake in my bed, I am at least able to distract my mind. I run through calculations on anticipated prices for this year's silk. I judge the chances of losing ships in storms. I plan mild revenges on the harbor master for his annual tax increases. And, when I feel I can bear the sadness, I open the gates to my memories of moments with you.

Remember the evening we evaded the guests at our own party and sneaked through the silent city to be alone on a hillside? Beneath the moonlight, we giggled not like a long-married couple but like teenagers. Remember how, at a passionate moment, the appearance of a herd of wild swine wandering the hillside sent us running?

I also remember a time when you fell asleep curled against me, with your hand on my chest and your face resting on your hand. When you woke—for I had been watching the rise and fall of your breathing—you blinked and lifted your head, and I saw the line of your rings in the skin of your lovely cheek. My heart burst to think that someone as beautiful as you would have accepted those rings as gifts from me.

Do you know what I worship most about your beauty? Your nose. The small freckles of perfection. The delicate curves. A profile of grace. How your nostrils flare during your quick surges of anger. It is a nose I can gaze upon for hours. Think me silly if you will, but I love your nose.

Now, this far from you, I am grateful for all the times early in our marriage when I woke in our chamber and silently watched you in the silvery moonlight, my near reverence as much for the beauty of your face surrounded by the hair draped on your pillow, as for the love inside me that would thicken my throat with sadness and joy and longing and gratitude.

Even now as I write, I smile, because for all your perfection in flesh and soul, it is not difficult to recall how thoroughly you have caused me vexation. I will remind you, as I have on many occasions, that a bath is not meant to take more time than the rebuilding of the temple. Nor was it intended by marriage vows that a husband be forced to pace for hours while his wife leisurely applies perfumes and chooses attire for a public occasion, all the while hearing assurances that the final result is but moments away.

But my smile fades, for I know I threw it all away. Even before the horror of the fire and your unspoken blame, I had lost much of the love you once gave me. Now, looking back, I see it happened in the way that dust settles. Slowly. Layer by layer.

How could I have been such a fool to let my ceaseless work become more important than my time for you and with you? Yet slowly, layer by layer, day by day as I pursued the wealth that would give us comfort in our old age, I was losing you. Worse, you even warned me many times, begging me to spend more time with you. All those days I threw away, days I could have idled hours with you and listened to you sing lullabies to our children.

Yet I spent my days at the harbor and at the warehouses. How could you not finally believe that gold was more important to me than your love?

Thinking of it, I sigh here in my lonely chamber. I long for you, more so for the final reason for our separation. I believe that I truly could win back the love we once had if not for that final, irrevocable event that put the chasm between us.

Yes, all of this remorse I carry and ponder during my wakeful state here.

Yet no sooner do I find the blessed relief of sleep, than the demons begin to hiss and coil around my unconscious soul. I do not dream, but instead see the startled wideness of our daughter's eyes, the fear on her face. I hear the screams of panic. I feel the panic and strength in her arms, as if once again she is clutching me in the throes of her agony. And then—as if once was not enough pain, must I be cursed with it again and again?—I see the flames. These details are inflicted on me so clearly that as she screams, I see flames licking at her oil-drenched skin. And I smell the scorch of tortured flesh. That smell brings me back to wakefulness, trembling and sweating and determined never to sleep again.

Pray for me, I beg. You embrace our Yahweh with far more devotion than I have ever shown him. I have distanced myself from any hope of mercy from him . . . pray for me.

9

The blind beggar cocked his head. In the early quiet of the city, before the priests even blew the trumpet calls to prayer, did he hear footsteps crossing the plaza?

Yes, his ears told him. *Coming from the west.*

The footsteps were soft. Slow. A man not in a hurry.

The footsteps belonged to me. The guest chamber had become too much of a prison. I had dressed quietly, trying to run from my memories by walking the city streets in the pale gray of the new light.

Later, I would come to know this man better. Well enough to guess that as I began to cross his path for the first time, he concentrated beyond the cramp of his hunger pains to visualize what his milky cataract-covered eyes could no longer tell him. He knew from memory the imposing sight presented by the temple behind him. Indeed, in his youth, he had been one of thousands of laborers who had worked on the massive reconstruction under Herod the Great. Each block of stone of the temple wall was almost the height of a man and easily several paces long. Hundreds of these blocks, piled hundreds of feet high, formed the massive walls. Here at the south entrance, two sets of wide steps led to the gates of the temple compound. In a few hours, it would be crowded with Passover pilgrims coming to make offerings, awed to stand in the temple's shadows.

Now, however, only he and I shared the vast plaza. The markets had yet to open, the wailing of public prayers had yet to begin, the wind had yet to rise.

The air was so quiet and still that the crowing of a cock easily crossed the valley from the top of the Mount of Olives.

As the first rays of the sun warmed the beggar's shoulders and ribs, he might have found it pleasant to sit and think of earlier days when a hard day's work was enough for bread and wine. Pleasant, except for his hunger. Except for his nervous tension. At this hour, he did not have the teeming public around him as protection. There was a strange intimacy in sharing this open empty place; how could he know what I might do to him, a helpless, blind old man?

My footsteps approached. Closer, closer. I was the total concern of his world.

My footsteps faded as I passed him by, telling him that his hopes and fears and past were worthless and insignificant to me. In anger, even more than from the need for money, the beggar rattled the two coins in his bowl.

I stopped and for the first time looked at him closely. His beard was streaked with gray and grease. His face was scarred and creased. He stank. Flies crawled across his rags.

I walked back toward him. He knew I was there.

The beggar stared straight ahead. Who was I? Soldier? Priest? Cruel? Kind? With just the two of us there in the plaza, I held power over him.

"I once was strong," the beggar said, speaking to me, the stranger he could not see. "Now I can no longer work. My wife died before I lost my sight, and we had no children to support us."

The beggar spoke simply, maintaining his dignity.

"You have not eaten in some days," I said. Did the beggar hear the accent in my voice? "There is a smell to a starving man. His body begins to burn impurities."

I knew this because my own fast had taken me almost to the point of death. What I had found interesting was that after the first week, my body lost its hunger. What I had found discouraging was that my self-imposed fast had not relieved the burden of my soul.

"I have not eaten in some days," the beggar acknowledged.

Undoubtedly, the beggar heard rustling as I opened my money purse. I poured coins into the bowl between his legs. After all, what did money matter to me?

"May God's peace rest upon you," the beggar said. From the shakiness in his voice, it seemed he might weep in gratitude.

"And upon you." But my mind was already elsewhere as I turned away.

I took a few steps. Then I realized he did not know me; I could speak to him without worrying about his opinion of me.

I returned and crouched beside the beggar.

"Tell me," I said. "If you were to die, what method would you chose?"

I saw him recoil in fear. There were men, of course, who killed simply for the pleasure of inflicting pain on another. For all the beggar knew, I was holding a knife. A sword. A length of rope. I could kill him swiftly, with no witnesses.

"Please," the beggar stuttered. "Keep your coins. I meant no offense by stopping you."

I laughed softly.

"I should ask your apology," I said. "I have startled you when I simply meant the question in a philosophical way. After all, if one attempts to discuss such things with friends, they become nervous. But you and I are here alone. You do not know me. I do not know you. Strange, how that makes it possible to share thoughts that would not be possible with someone you knew."

I paused. "So tell me, what do you think is the least painful way to die? My own opinion is that the Romans do it best. They sit in a steam bath and open a vein. Death approaches as a faintness that comes with the loss of blood. Of course, the mess is very inconsiderate to those left behind."

The beggar relaxed somewhat. This *was* an eerie topic to discuss.

"There is, however, the matter of the obvious sin of taking one's own life," I continued. "Especially with the iron rod of Moses and his commandments hanging over one. So instead should a man attempt to deceive those close to him? Perhaps a fight might work best. One could throw himself into battle against Roman soldiers. This would give the appearance of a heroic death. God himself might be fooled into believing it was not suicide. And a wife . . ."

I sighed. "A wife, too, might find it at least forgivable."

"If it's only a woman's opinion that concerns you," the beggar said, "I would give it no more thought. If she loves you, no method of death would be forgiven. If she doesn't love you, any death will suffice, as long as you leave behind enough to attract the next suitor."

I thought about his words. From the lower part of Jerusalem, we heard the first arguments of vendors at the market as they set up their wares.

"Well spoken," I finally said. "You have responded well to a question designed to amuse me."

Before the beggar could reply, I straightened and walked away. What troubled me most was wondering whether I had meant my question for more than amusement.

10

It would be a wishful twist of memory to say with certainty that I noticed Yeshua and his disciples as they journeyed to Jerusalem early in the day.

Yet, for all I know, I could well have seen them. Again, a need for solitude had drawn me from the city. In the country-side, the sunshine and solitude gave my soul the illusion of freedom.

But it was only an illusion.

Resting on a large boulder on the side of the hill, I gazed at the faraway road that led down the Mount of Olives; the burden that had weighed heavily upon me for the previous eighteen months stayed squarely with me.

To Pascal—when we sat down to complete our transaction—I would give the truth. A fire had destroyed one of my warehouses. I was tired of business.

Yet, I would not tell him the entire truth: that my wife had only coldness in her heart, that my daughter recoiled from my touch, that I had discovered far too late what was truly valuable.

As to my intentions once Pascal and I came to terms and I had ensured the well-being of my family, I was still unsure. I wondered whether I could find comfort in a quiet life in some

far corner of the empire. I also realized there was another possibility, which was frightening me less and tempting me more.

Deep in such thoughts, I would barely have paid attention
to the pilgrims as they descended the Mount of Olives. Of
course, at that time I did not know Yeshua stayed in Bethany
each night, nor did I care that he was determined to return to
Jerusalem each new day.

Still, had I actually been looking, I might have seen Yeshua
and his followers among the stream of pilgrims. Had I
noticed, however, I still would not have understood why they
stopped near a fig tree. Or what that stop would mean to the
one named Judas Iscariot. . . .

Halfway down the Mount of Olives, the unseasonably
early leaves of a solitary fig tree were obvious from a considerable distance. While shrubs and wildflowers had begun
to emerge, dotting the hillsides with color, the season had
yet to woo anything but the fig tree into such a luxurious
cloak of green. It stood in welcome contrast to the rocky soil
around it.

Judas, however, had no eye for the beauty of the wild hills
or the oasis of shade the fig tree promised. Of all the disciples,
he walked farthest behind the teacher. Inside his purse, the fingers of his right hand played with layers of shekels as he
sought relief for his uneasiness, which felt like black blood
coursing through his veins.

He'd brought up the rear of the small procession since
they'd left Bethpage, shuffling his sandals at an unenthusias-
tic pace with little energy. The crisp air of the morning had
not roused his spirits; rather it seemed the cheerfulness of the
pale blue sky and a sun not yet hot, along with the promise of

a new season in the beginning bloom of wild flowers, all served to taunt him for the darkness his soul could not shake.

He'd slept poorly, waking again and again to remember pieces of his short conversation with the stranger in the crowd.

Why has he not taken the cloak of Messiah?

In Capernaum, he commanded them not to rise up against the Romans . . . nothing noble about drowning unnecessarily, particularly if power is to be found elsewhere.

Should you ever want to know, you may find me among the Sanhedrists. Those who hold true power.

Those statements worked like a slow poison, and when Judas felt guilt at his traitorous thoughts, he washed the guilt away with anger. After all, Yeshua had the entire world at his command. If he did not act upon it, should Judas be blamed for the natural result of resentment?

He was so deep into his bitter contemplation that when the procession stopped, he stumbled into Peter, striking him squarely between the shoulder blades.

Judas blinked. The small group had bunched at the side of the road. He saw no reason for the sudden halt.

"What's this?" Peter joked, spinning to see Judas. "A blind sparrow flutters against my neck?"

Some of the others laughed at Peter's affectionate remark.

Judas raised his lips in a smile to hide his thoughts. Earlier, Judas had fooled himself into believing such jokes were meant to include him. Now he knew differently. Had not the teacher deliberately excluded him earlier—taking only Peter, James, and John up to a mountain one night for meditation? Inside, Judas flamed with anger at where his thoughts began to take him. After all the work he had done, after all he had given of his life over the past three years. . . .

Again, Peter interrupted Judas's thoughts, grabbing him by the elbow, fully expecting this unspoken imperious Galilean command to focus his attention. Judas frowned in irritation. More and more the arrogant fisherman was taking a position as second-in-command. Had they forgotten Judas was the one trusted with the band's funds?

Nonetheless, Judas turned his attention to where Peter pointed. Yeshua was walking a delicate path through low thorny bushes.

"It's a fig he wants," Peter said.

So now, Judas thought with scorn, *the fisherman knows the teacher's thoughts?*

Yeshua stopped at the base of the tree and looked up into its wide branches.

"As we left this morning, some of us warned him to break his fast," Peter said softly. "It was plain that a night of prayer had worn him into a faint of hunger. But he insisted on leaving for Jerusalem."

"It is not the season for figs," Judas said. Yeshua was still searching the tree. "Surely he knows that."

"You have a head good with figures," Peter said with a smile. "But it is easy to guess that you are not from the country. See the tree's greenness? It is well known in Galilee that the fruit on a fig always appears before the leaves. Failing that, there should be old fruit from last season, just as edible as new fruit. Don't be surprised when our master finds a fig."

Yeshua walked several steps around the tree's trunk, growing more impatient as he pushed apart leaves in his search.

"Thank you for increasing my limited education," Judas replied. "How I ever lived without such knowledge is beyond me."

Peter did not hear the sarcasm and patted Judas on the shoulder. Before, Judas would have accepted such an action with a glow of fellowship. Now it seemed condescending.

Beneath the tree, Yeshua gave up his search and picked his way back through the brush.

"Barren," Peter said quietly. "In any man's garden, it would only be good for kindling."

"Again," Judas said, taking satisfaction in his ambiguous tone, "I thank you for your valuable teaching. It will undoubtedly serve me well in my own orchards."

Judas enjoyed Peter's response, a quick strange look as if the big man had finally suspected something amiss but did not have the intelligence to understand.

Peter's jaw began to move—Judas nearly laughed at the thought that the fisherman was so slow he needed to have his mouth in motion to think—but his reply was interrupted by the teacher. He surprised them all by speaking his first words of the day's journey not to them, but to the tree.

"May no one ever eat fruit from you again," Yeshua said, then he turned toward Jerusalem.

His followers also turned and exchanged puzzled looks. Not even Judas—ever alert for hidden meaning in any man's words—could make sense of the teacher's utterance, for his tone had been completely flat.

Judas had, of course, noticed one thing. In the intimacy of sharing shrugs, none of the other eleven—Galileans, when he was Judean—had bothered to glance at him.

Judas decided he would remember that. Just as he remembered all the injustices in his life.

11

To my surprise, on my return to the city, I saw the blind beggar again. He was not begging but awkwardly shuffling through the temple.

To enter the city, I had done what most who arrived from the direction of Jericho did. Instead of taking the longer route past the Pool of Bethesda and around the north side of the temple, I came through the east gate, which allowed me to cut directly through the temple to the lower quarters of Jerusalem on the other side. The bedlam of the moneychangers and livestock in the temple had hardly distracted me. But when I caught a glimpse of the man shuffling uncertainly with people moving quickly around him, I stopped. Twice, as I watched, uncaring pedestrians knocked him to his knees.

I'm not sure what moved me to help him. Perhaps it was the pitiful sight of someone struggling to reach a destination he could not see. Perhaps I felt somewhat the role of his guardian; I had already assisted him with a gift of gold. Or perhaps seeing his misery was a balm to my own. Regardless, I reached him quickly and took him by the elbow.

"Don't be alarmed," I told him at his startled flinch. "We spoke this morning."

He recognized my voice and smiled toothlessly as he lifted his face toward me. Then he frowned.

"I cannot return your money," he said quickly with a shiver of fear. "It is—"

"I am not here for the coins," I said. Passersby jostled us. The din was so loud I was forced to lean into his ear. The smell of his unwashed body and clothing caused me to regret this closeness. "Rather, I offer assistance. Where do you wish to go? And what madness has you venturing into the temple crowd?"

At first, I did not believe I heard correctly. Not with the shouting of moneychangers, the noise of livestock, and the ceaseless noise of bartering. I asked him to repeat his words.

"I want to see!" he shouted. "I have heard that the prophet has arrived again. If I find him, he can heal me!"

Did I want to be party to this beggar's disappointment? After all, even if we actually found the prophet among the thousands in the temple, the only certainty awaiting this old, blind man was tomorrow's blindness. Not healing.

However, as we stood, the prophet and his followers approached us. Although I witnessed what happened next, I later heard it retold in complaint—as I hid my smile and pretended ignorance—from a friend of Pascal, a friend who had a far greater stake in the event than I had. . . .

12

Oren, son of Judd, stood hardly taller than the heads of the goats in the enclosure behind him. His robes were of fine woven cloth, and his fingers heavy with thick rings of gold. What did it matter that the stench of manure clung to his shoes, or that he was often covered with the dirt of livestock? He was a man of power.

Oren had earned his wealth over the years in the same way he was earning it at the moment—examining sacrificial animals, priding himself on his ability to focus even when the pace of commerce was at its most hectic and demanding during the madness of Passover.

Around him, filling the Court of the Gentiles, thousands of pilgrims streamed past the animal enclosures and money tables creating a babble of noise punctuated by merchants' shouts and children's cries. Cramped against each other in their respective pens, lambs and goats and oxen and cattle milled nervous circles; the smell of fresh dung scattered by their hooves was ample proof of their instinctive fear of the unaccustomed din.

Dozens of pilgrims waited sullenly for Oren to inspect their offerings—small lambs tucked under arms, goats led by ropes, doves in reed cages. An old woman with a lamb stood directly before Oren.

He turned the lamb upside down and frowned at a spot on its belly.

"Impure," he announced to the elderly woman. "Not fit for sacrifice."

"What's that?" She cupped her ears with her hands, trying to hear above the din.

"I cannot give my approval to an animal with blemishes," he said, knowing she was too dim-sighted to realize the spot was merely dirt. He could clean the lamb later and sell it for great profit. "Without my approval, the priests will not accept it at the altar."

"I brought my best lamb," she protested. "It cannot be blemished."

"Ignorance like yours is why the priests engage a *mumcheh* like me."

"I am offering God the best I have!" She was close to weeping.

Oren shrugged. "Have you spent a year and a half with a farmer learning what faults are temporary and what faults are permanent?"

"No, but—"

"I have. The priest will take my word over yours." He held out his hand. "I have been authorized to charge six isar for my judgment."

Oren clucked self-righteously. "You could have avoided this trouble and bought your animal at the market here."

"From thieves who ask for a pigeon the price of a month's food?"

Again, he shrugged. "Do you wish the inconvenience of

carrying this impure lamb or do wish to leave it with me to dispose of for you?"

At this final outrage, the elderly woman lost her patience. "I traveled three weeks to get here. I paid two denarii to change my coins to shekels for the temple tribute. And you propose to steal the very lamb you have rejected?"

Oren's thick ruddy lips formed a waxen smile. "You are welcome to have another *mumcheh* examine your lamb. For another six isar, of course."

The elderly woman screeched with anger. "You are all thieves! Working together to squeeze blood from our bones! If I were a man I would—"

Voices behind her rose in agreement. Until louder shouts distracted them.

"The prophet! He arrives! It is Yeshua, from Nazareth!"

Oren hoped they were wrong.

Then he heard a roar of approval. Although suspicion told him what to expect, he needed to see for himself. Oren remembered very clearly a time when Yeshua had visited before. Oren had been one of the prophet's first victims. He had no intention of seeing his money scattered again.

Oren groaned with effort and somehow squirmed his fat body onto his table. The table sagged. He tottered as he stretched to look over the crowd. What he saw confirmed his dread. The lunatic from Nazareth had begun another rampage.

13

From my vantage point, one hand still firmly clasping the blind beggar's elbow, I saw everything clearly. And with some degree of fascination.

The prophet Yeshua was less than a dozen steps away.

He showed no anger. Instead, great resolve was etched into his face. Already, he had turned over two money tables. Shekels and pagan coins had scattered like grain; the money-changers were on their hands and knees, trying to scoop the coins together.

The next table held cages of doves. Had he wrenched the table on its side, the doves would have been crushed. Instead, Yeshua leaned on the table and stared at the much taller, angry merchant behind it.

But the stare was enough. Instead of shouting, the man snapped his jaw shut and stepped away. With quick flicks of his fingers, the prophet opened the cage doors. Blossoms of white freedom, the doves whirred into the air above the crowd.

Yeshua upended two more money tables in silence. Several moneychangers down the line had lifted their tunics by the hems with one hand, uncaring of the indignity of exposing their skinny white legs as they scrambled to throw coins into the makeshift pouches. Despite their frantic efforts, they were not fast enough and fell backward as Yeshua flipped their tables.

He stopped abruptly and spun toward the gates of the animal enclosures. Pulling open the gates of the goat pen first, he waded in, waving his arms to drive the goats into the crowd. Then the cattle, the sheep and lambs, and finally the oxen.

The animals did much of the remaining work, knocking over tables and benches, bumping into merchants so greedy to guard their money that they refused to move away from the stampede of frightened beasts.

Around me, the confusion multiplied as people panicked. Twice I had to pull the blind beggar from the path of oxen. People flowed around us, at first trying to stem the escape of livestock, then fleeing it. Sheep, goats, and oxen barged in all directions.

The blind beggar kept crying for an explanation of the noise and confusion around him. I shouted to him to stay with me and wait. I did not know it at the time, of course, but the chaos had extended far beyond this portion of the temple.

Above all of it, I could hear pilgrims cheer. They thrilled to watch Yeshua's righteous anger. This man dared to stand alone against corruption. While the pilgrims needed animals for sacrifice at the altar, a proper market had been established on the lower portion of the Mount of Olives. The family of Annas had no scriptural authority for its stranglehold on these tainted profits.

Yeshua's moral certainty, like a physical force, at first made the merchants fall away. Then, as his methodical action gained momentum, the crowd's approval of his stance against the thievery was too much for any one merchant to overcome.

Still, as Yeshua continued, I could not help but wonder when the temple police would arrive.

I can thank Pascal and his love for passing on gossip from his well-to-do customers for the answer I eventually discovered. . . .

When the first priests reached Caiaphas, the high priest, they were out of breath. It had been a long run from the Court of the Gentiles.

Caiaphas turned from conversation with a chief priest and raised his eyebrows in question at the noisy approach of the two men.

"He is at the money tables," one gasped. He waved his arms in a rapid gesture of confusion. "The animals! Coins! Benches everywhere! Send the temple police!"

Caiaphas froze him by raising a single bony finger.

"Do not ever tell me what to do." Tall and angular, with a reach as wide as a vulture's wingspan, Caiaphas caused some to say his face mirrored the wrathful countenance of God. Caiaphas prided himself on the image and was as miserly with his smiles as with his shekels.

Confronted by his full anger, the second Pharisee actually twitched in fear and tried to suck back his own sobs for air, hoping not to be noticed.

Caiaphas looked back and forth between them until he was satisfied at their level of terror.

"Tell me," Caiaphas said. "Is the crowd in favor of his actions?"

Both nodded.

"Then we do nothing," Caiaphas announced. He glanced over their shoulders at the tower of Fort Antonia, where six hundred Roman soldiers were garrisoned and ready to quell any public riots.

Caiaphas closed his eyes. He spoke softly, more to himself than to the others: "This is not our time. When our time arrives, it will be formed at our choosing, without the people around to protect him."

14

The animals left behind fallen tables, the litter of empty money bowls, merchants searching for coins on the ground, empty stock pens, and near silence. In that silence the crowd watched a man lift high one final dove cage.

Somehow, although the gesture was plainly symbolic, Yeshua did not appear theatrical as he released the latch on the cage.

The dove burst skyward, its wings audible in the vast open area.

Yeshua looked at the crowd and called out a text I recognized from Isaiah. "It is written in the Scriptures, 'My Temple will be called a house for prayer for people from all nations.'"

He paused and surveyed the remaining merchants. "But you," he called out again, "are changing God's house into a hideout for robbers."

Behind me, in the quiet that followed the man's echoing words, I heard the tap-tap of a stick on stone. I turned my head to see the uncertain progress of a stooped and twisted cripple, his head covered with rags.

"Heal me," the man begged, weeping. "Oh Lord, let me walk again."

"Where," my blind beggar groaned as he heard the other man, "where is the prophet now? Point me to where he is and let me go."

All focus centered on the cripple, who was undaunted by the crowd with all its stares. I told myself my own rapt attention was intellectual curiosity. The rumors of miracles, could they be true?

The blind beggar tried to pull himself from my grasp. I held tight. Somehow, this moment had dignity. Even at my most cynical and weary, I would find no humor in watching a blind beggar race against a cripple.

With gentle grace, Yeshua moved to meet the crippled man. He took him by the hand and led him toward the inner courts of the temple.

"Let me take you to him," I said to the blind beggar.

I followed with the crowd, guiding the beggar, who clutched my arm with hands that quivered in hope and excitement.

15

At the evening meal, Pascal was still dressed in the fine clothing he had worn during the day. Seraphine had tied her hair back, and it added a beauty to her face that surprised me and brought me some sadness, for it reminded me of the beauty in my own wife's face.

The wide assortment of food arrayed on the table before us looked no different from the table of the previous evening. Pascal's hospitality was generous, partly because tradition demanded it of a host, partly because of his affection for me, and partly, I suspect with no cruelty, because he always wanted me to be keenly aware of his status and wealth.

As with the night before, I remained quiet. Less from weariness than from shock. I had left the temple in a daze so profound that I did not remember the steep climb along the streets to Pascal's mansion, nor the details of giving my cloak to the servant who greeted me at the door.

To this point in the meal, Pascal had made no mention of my earlier offer to sell my entire estate, nor had he questioned why I had not visited him during the day to discuss it further. While the matter was probably uppermost in his mind, Seraphine's presence again kept us from talking business.

"You drive Seraphine to tears," Pascal said to break the

long silence that had fallen around the table. I had yet to say a single word; their forced conversation had brought the meal this far. "Please, eat, drink. Seraphine's beginning to think you have no respect for her efforts."

"Cripples walked," I said, hardly a response that either might have expected. "Blind men saw."

There. I had said it aloud. I still could barely believe what my eyes had forced upon my mind. By speaking it, fully expecting wild crazed laughter as response, I had taken the first step toward accepting it.

"What?" Pascal's beard was soaked with grease, his mouth half full of bread. He gestured with the chicken leg in his hand, waving it to get Seraphine's attention. "My cousin's first words of the meal, and he sounds drunk. Yet I have not seen him taste any wine."

"Cripples walked," I said. "Blind men saw. I was there."

They had approached him in the afternoon sunlight in the courtyard of the temple. He had spoken to them softly, one at a time. Then he had bent his face toward them, listening intently to their replies. Never before had I seen such compassion on a man's face, such naked love for the weak, the ugly, the infirm. Then—and my body still trembled to think of it—he had laid his hands upon their afflicted limbs. And somehow, the stooped straightened, the crippled dropped their canes. At his command, the blind turned their faces to the sun and blinked at the light, tears streaming down their cheeks. Children had danced, singing hosannas that not even the temple authorities could silence, reaching for heaven with their souls, their sweet voices ringing off the high temple walls like the distant melody of angels.

He had healed them.

Nothing in my entire life had prepared me for this. It was as if I had seen objects fall up, not down.

He had healed them.

"Come, come," Pascal said. "Explain this nonsense."

"The prophet from Galilee. The one they say raised a man from the dead. At the temple today, he overturned the money tables, ran the thieving traders out of the market. He—"

"Yes, yes," Pascal said, grinning. He paused to drink deeply from his wine cup. His eyes shone in the flickering oil light. "I heard of that business. I wish I could have seen it! They tell me it was chaos. Men and beasts everywhere. I wonder if tomorrow the market will be shut down or if—"

I slammed an open palm down on the table in sudden rage.

"Listen to me!" I roared. "He . . . healed . . . them!"

I found myself half-standing, looking down the table at Pascal and Seraphine. They stared back at me with their mouths open wide. Pascal had wanted to treat the entire matter as a trivial joke, yet he had no understanding that merely thinking of what I had seen was enough to make me feel as if I were swaying on the edge of the world. How could it be that a man healed cripples and blind men by touching them? It defied logic, the one strength I had learned to use as my foundation for life.

He had healed them.

I wanted to weep in my confusion. Slowly, the emotion that had driven me to my feet drained away.

I sat.

"Forgive me," I said. "This day has been a strain."

Like the well-mannered hosts they were, my cousin and his wife continued the conversation politely, as if my outburst had not occurred.

"So, you were in the temple today," Pascal said after some small talk, nodding with a smile of cultivated interest.

"Pascal," I said, hardly trusting my voice, "I saw the prophet touch them. He healed them. Had you been there, you would be just as afraid as I am."

"Afraid?" It was probably the first time he had heard me admit fear.

"It is not rational," I said. "That he could touch a cripple and cause him to walk is not rational. If I had not been there, I wouldn't believe it. And, frankly, I don't expect you to believe it from me. But I saw it. He healed them."

I could not get my mind away from that one thought. *He had healed them.*

"Well," Pascal said, "in philosophical terms, I agree with you. Men are notoriously fickle and will only believe what they want to believe. Were I an ignorant peasant with little hope beyond far-fetched stories, I would desperately want to believe you. And so my belief would be certain. But I am not a peasant. I have carved my own comfortable place in the world. My range of experiences and education do not put me in a position where I need to clutch at desperate hope. So, no—and do not take this as an insult—I don't believe you."

"I don't want to believe it myself," I said. "Because then I would have to accept that there are things beyond my understanding."

"Exactly." Pascal took a fried locust, regarded it briefly with satisfaction, and popped it into his mouth. "Dear cousin, let me comfort you."

I waited for him to finish chewing. He washed the mouthful down with more wine.

"You see," he said. "Rumors of this man and his so-called

wonders have come to us for nearly three years. We are not provincials, willing to accept any type of hearsay. Everything he has done can be explained easily if you realize he is just another messianic fraud. It is simple to 'heal' a cripple who was never crippled in the first place. Bring in strangers on canes, wave your hand, and send them on their way—healed. And well-paid, of course."

"Why?" I asked. "Why go to all that trouble?"

"Influence. Once you have a great enough following, you have power. Whatever he did in the temple today was show-manship timed to impress the pilgrims at Passover. Most of them come from small towns, far away, and are ready to believe anything as a miracle."

Pascal shook his head. "This Lazarus. All he had to do was sneak into a tomb and wait there until called forth a few days later. Those who believe a dead man walked again are fools who deserve to lose whatever money they spend on his cause."

"I haven't heard the prophet ask for money," I said.

"Once he has power, the money will follow. Any man shrewd enough to be as patient as he appears knows that."

Pascal smiled. "You see, this Nazarene might have a fol-lowing outside of Jerusalem, but here in the city, among those who count, he is nothing."

Pascal set down his well-gnawed chicken bone and stared at me. "Consider this a mild warning," he said. "But any man who wishes to do business in Jerusalem must consider his reputation. One who is linked to the rebel will find few to sup-port him. Even those who might wish to do business with him would face pressure from others to shun the follower."

I understood. It was far from a mild warning. Pascal would not be able to involve himself with me or my business if I did something as foolhardy as publicly join the throng at Yeshua's feet.

Pascal dropped his voice to a conspiratorial whisper. "As I told you yesterday, that man is in danger. Trust me; I know this from those who count. The matter will be taken care of shortly."

Later, alone with my thoughts in the guest chamber, I desperately wanted to believe Pascal—that Yeshua was a magician, a fraud, a messianic impostor like dozens who had tried the same before him. It was easier to not believe than to believe.

Yet . . .

There was the blind old beggar who I had guided to the prophet. Because I had seen the same blind beggar before in the temple plaza, I doubted he was an actor hired by Yeshua. And when I left the old man this afternoon, his eyes were no longer milky with cataracts, but shiny with tears of joy.

I lay down on the bed but did not expect to sleep. For the eighteen months since the fire in my warehouse, that luxury had been denied me—except in short stretches when my body's needs overcame my sorrow and horror. The most impoverished peasants slept deeply while I, with all my gold, could not buy a single night's sleep.

It was an irony that had long since failed to amuse me.

As the lonely wakeful hours passed, my mind kept returning to the prophet and the people I had seen him heal.

What if Pascal were wrong? What if—against everything rational—this man truly could heal the afflicted? It would skew my entire view of the world.

It took a long while for another thought to push its way to

the surface, probably because for too many months I had believed there could be no solution for my problems.

If this man truly had the power to heal—in some way I could not fathom—he could heal my daughter's legs.

And if there was hope for her, was there then hope for me?

Hope was something that had become so foreign that I barely recognized it. When it arrived, shining a light where darkness had reigned so long, I began to weep.

At that moment, I realized what I had kept hidden from myself the entire journey here—I desperately wanted not to die alone, far away from my family.

TUESDAY

16

My dearest love,

I promised I would write to you as if I were courting you again. I have been speaking to you from my heart. I cannot continue honestly without admitting to the mistresses who drove us apart over the years.

My first mistress, of course, was ambition. Now, as I contemplate what a man's life is worth, I see the futility of pursuing power and wealth. When I am gone, those accomplishments will be divided and fought over by other men who also vainly pursue the emptiness. They will also someday feel the disappointment of discovering that all they have managed to grasp is a meaningless bubble on the waves of an eternal tide.

What is worth more than gold?

Your love, freely given. The love of our sweet daughter instead of the legacy of horror that is her inheritance. And, more than anything, the life of our son.

I have failed you all. Now I understand too clearly how my actions have hurt you, how the pain continues to mold you. Truly, the stones a man casts send ripples through time; the spirit of a man and the love that he gave, or did not give, continue in his children and their children long after his wealth and power have disappeared.

Perhaps this is something I have known all along but could not admit to myself. For as I look back, I see how the empty promise of that first mistress led me to seek solace in the arms of a second.

Let us not pretend she did not exist. Let us not pretend I did not serve her willingly. Let us not pretend she was not my escape.

It may have been better for you if this second mistress had been another woman. No other woman could have competed with your beauty and charm. If you still had some affection for me, you could easily have banished such a temptation from my life.

But the solace of wine is like none other. Cares disappear, and in the glow of well-being the spirit seems to become full where it was empty.

That you kept our household in some semblance of order during those months of constant drink is a testimony to your strength. I would ask your forgiveness if I thought I deserved it. I would pursue redemption if I thought it possible.

You have never blamed me aloud, but I always know it is there. The night of the fire, you think I could have done more. You are right in blaming me, yet also wrong. The truth of that evening is why I am now in Jerusalem, fleeing you.

Yet today, my love, I go forth with small hope when yesterday I saw nothing but goodbye.

I make this promise.

If, somehow, through this ridiculous hope that I clutch as fiercely as breath itself, I find a way to give our daughter back her legs, I will return to you. I will read these letters aloud to you myself. You will hear the truth about the fire from me, not a servant who delivers these letters with word that I am out of your life, never to return.

Then, and only then, will I get on my knees and beg you to allow us to begin anew.

17

I did not go early into the countryside as I had on previous days. I intended to seek solace in another way and had even begun to hope that I might not sell my estate to Pascal.

So it was that I found myself walking directly to the temple, hoping the prophet might return.

Broken clouds sent shadows drifting across the great plaza at the south end of the temple. A quickening breeze promised rain later. I felt the chill and pulled my cloak tighter around my body.

Although it was early and the monstrous temple gates were still closed, as many as two hundred people had already gathered in the plaza, standing in clusters as they gossiped or alone as they set up assorted wares on blankets to sell to pilgrims later in the day. Still, because of the vastness of the plaza, it seemed empty.

At a distance, I had no difficulty picking out the one person I could recognize. The blind beggar I had met the day before. Except he was no longer blind.

I knew he would not recognize me; I had led him close to Yeshua and, before his vision returned, had retreated to lose myself in the temple crowd.

I watched him for several minutes without approaching.

Other ragged beggars—crippled, blind, old—had begun to take their regular positions near the temple gates armed with canes and bowls. Soon, when the thousands upon thousands of pilgrims streamed into the plaza, the beggars' clamor and wailing would add to the general din of temple activities.

My beggar—I smiled faintly when I realized I thought of him in this manner—walked from one to another, stooping as he talked to each. His back was to me, and I was too far away to clearly see his actions, but I could guess them by the excitement he left behind each time he moved to another beggar.

I walked closer and confirmed my guess. The man I had given gold to the day before was now handing it to the other beggars.

I stood in front of him.

He flicked his eyes up and down my body. Briefly, I wondered if he recognized me. Perhaps he had not been blind and was indeed a part of a trick by Yeshua.

Then I decided his interest might be from the joy of registering as many tiny details as he could. He took in my luxurious clothing and my expensive cloak. His eyes stopped briefly on the scar of my face. Other men might have grown their beards longer to cover such a reminder. I would not.

"Shalom," I said.

He recognized—or pretended to recognize—my voice. "It is you!"

I nodded.

He reached out and clasped my right hand, shaking it vigorously. In close quarters, I did not smell the unwashed odor that had clung to him the day before. His clothes were not expensive, but new. And he had trimmed his beard.

"I cannot thank you enough," he said. "You led me to the Messiah."

Uncomfortable, I pried my hand loose.

"I see you are dispensing money as if you are Solomon himself."

"Yes, yes," he said. His voice was as animated as his movements. This man could not contain himself. "I feel as if I am Solomon."

"Where will you find shekels tomorrow?" I asked. "And the day after?"

"With the gifts I have received, how can I think merely of myself? Others here have greater need. Of all people, I should know how keen that need is."

His answer shamed me. *Would a paid actor have done this?* I smiled to cover my shame.

"What is your name?" he asked. "I am Nahshon. My family has been in Jerusalem since before the Romans."

It occurred to me that I had been content to think of him as "my beggar." With a name and this meager information, I was now forced to acknowledge him as more than an object of pity. This was the danger of helping people directly instead of helping charity.

"I am Simeon," I said. "My family has roots in Alexandria." I saw little need to tell him how I had struck out on my own after my youth in the harbor, and where it had taken me since then.

"You are a young man," he said. His eyes flicked briefly back to my scar. "Wife? Children?"

My natural inclination is silence; I'm often too busy to worry about the niceties of everyday conversation. But because this man was a stranger with whom I'd already been candid, and because of my emotional rawness, I did not retreat into privacy as I would have normally.

"I have a wife," I said. "And a daughter—Vashti."

Jaala and I had called our daughter Vashti because the name meant "fairest, loveliest woman"; now her name served as cruel mockery of what she would never be.

"I will pray that God will bless you with a son," Nahshon said, on the assumption that any man would proudly mention a son before a daughter.

I kept my face a blank. We had called our son Ithnan—the strong sailor. One who was to inherit my ships, my warehouses, my shops. One who had laughed as he ran, taking pleasure in the motion of his sturdy little legs.

"My young son died recently in a fire," I said.

I touched the scar on my face. "It was the same fire that gave me this." I was acutely aware of how the scar pulled with certain expressions—a constant reminder of that horrid day.

Nahshon's eyes widened. But not for the reasons I expected.

"Yesterday, you took me to the Messiah when you could have stood in my place to beg for mercy. You are a kind and selfless man! I will pray for you in your grief."

I could not tell this joy-filled man that it had not been selflessness that had kept me from the Messiah, but lack of faith.

"How long had you been blind?" I asked, weary of talking about myself.

He was more than eager to answer. I learned about his time as a temple worker. And his now-dead wife. And the years between.

I cut his enthusiasm short a few minutes later.

"What did you feel?" I asked, aching to understand. If Nahshon were a hired actor, pretending blindness in the morning and new vision in the afternoon, he was well worth any money a false Messiah had paid him. "What was it like?"

"I felt silvery light," he said without any hesitation. As if all that had occupied his mind was that moment of healing. "I did not see it, but I felt it. Like a bright star alone in a dark sky, growing brighter and warmer until it filled the heavens. When he took his hand from my eyes, the star's warm light became the sun; I could see it shining down on the temple. . . . And peace. I felt peace. No words can explain the strength of that peace."

I closed my eyes briefly, wishing against all knowledge that I could believe this man before me.

"He may return today," Nahshon said. "Go to him. He can heal you!"

We both knew the unspoken. Yeshua could not give me back my son.

I shook my head.

"My daughter was burned in the fire that took my son. It is she who needs healing," I answered. "I do not."

18

Nahshon, old as he was, sparkled with the exuberance of a boy. I easily saw that in his renewed joy, he wanted to be moving, exploring. It soon became apparent that a sense of obligation kept him in further conversation with me.

I offered him an excuse, pleading business of my own, and sent him free.

By then, the temple doors had opened. I joined the crowd moving inside, hoping to see the man of miracles.

My hope was not in vain. As I learned later, he was delayed only briefly on his journey from Bethany to Jerusalem. . . .

On their descent of the Mount of Olives, Peter, of all the disciples, saw it first. Where once green had softened the outline of the fig tree, a framework of drooping branches now showed through leaves turned brown, curled, and dry, rustling in the breeze.

"Yeshua, look!" Peter cried. "The fig tree you cursed has withered!"

Peter's large hands flailed as the words tumbled from his mouth, his excitement so great that he shared his news with the other disciples as if they could not see for themselves.

"Yesterday. Remember? The teacher spoke to the tree. Did you not hear? He said that no one would ever eat fruit from it again. And look! It's withered."

With the scorn that the cynical use as a defense against enthusiasm, Judas rolled his eyes as Peter continued to point.

"To its roots," Peter said. "Look. Withered to its roots. Just as the teacher commanded and more!"

"Tell me, Peter," Judas said, sounding like an adult patronizing a child. "Has something happened to the tree?"

"Yes, yes," Peter said. He was too caught up in the marvel to hear Judas's tone. "Overnight! The tree has died. See for yourself."

Judas looked around to see if the others enjoyed the humor of his sarcasm. He felt doubly pleased by Peter's oblivion to it. But none of the other disciples paid Judas attention. Of late, they'd grown accustomed to his sourness. Besides, Judas's attempt at attention paled beside what their eyes beheld. The tree had actually died overnight at the mere words of their teacher.

"Master," Peter said, slowing down, "the tree . . ."

Yeshua continued to walk. Often he would not answer until a time of silence and contemplation had passed. They had almost come abreast of the tree when Yeshua spoke.

"Have faith in God," Yeshua answered, pausing deliberately.

Would they understand? Without faith, Israel in its appearance of glory was as barren of God as the tree had been of figs. And whatever resisted God would most surely be swept away.

Yeshua waited for a glimmering of comprehension, but the faces around him remained rapt with awe. The miracle itself had impressed them. A storm calmed, the lame healed, a man raised from the dead. In all of it, as with the withered fig tree, they had failed to look beyond.

The common rabbinical expression for doing the impossible was "rooting up mountains," and as a Jewish teacher, Yeshua gave his followers the comfort of the familiar in his attempt to lead them further.

"I tell you the truth," Yeshua continued, "you can say to this mountain, 'Go, fall into the sea.' And if you have no doubts in your mind and believe that what you say will happen, God will do it for you."

Still he faced the blank, rapt awe of children. Should it not be obvious? Faith not only gives power to prayer but is also its foundation. He had, on another occasion, told them the two great laws of faith: love God, love man. True prayer then demands thoughts that glorify God in those two ways. True prayer demands by extension a spirit untainted by selfish ambition or unforgiveness. Could they not see? In true prayer, a man bound to earth can reach up to heaven. Such is faith.

Yet Yeshua did not show any frustration. He smiled at his listeners. These men had traveled with him for three years and shared his pains, joys, hopes, sorrows, and disappointments. They were young, unlearned. Any teaching he shared could only be an outpouring of love and compassion.

"So I tell you," he said quietly to complete his words, "to believe that you have received the things you ask for in prayer, and God will give them to you. When you are praying, if you are angry with someone, forgive him so that your Father in heaven will also forgive your sins."

Would they understand? With faith, they could have everything. Without faith, whatever resisted God would most surely be swept away.

Yeshua, still smiling, looked from one face to another.

When his eyes met those of Judas, the slender disciple flinched and looked away.

One of the twelve, it seemed, understood too well the judgment against the fig tree that had denied Yeshua.

19

Although I had been waiting in a corner of the courtyard, when Yeshua arrived I did not approach him or his disciples. Not many pilgrims had arrived yet, but there were enough that I could remain among them and watch without being noticed.

The clouds had begun to thicken. With the breeze came an occasional waft of incense, reaching my nostrils like an unseen butterfly moving randomly through the air.

I had not minded the wait. Hope was so precious, I was reluctant to test it. And, with the habits of business I could not escape, I preferred to size up my prospective client.

As I watched, Yeshua laughed and joked with his followers and the few pilgrims who sat on the outer edges of the group.

I found myself liking this man. He had entered this lion's den of his own free will, knowing his very presence would be a challenge to the religious authorities. Yet he did not tread lightly as if fearing to wake the lions, nor did he posture with bluff braveness as a man with a sword, daring the lions to attack.

He was relaxed, handsome when he smiled. Yet, unlike some attractive men, he did not have the oiliness that repels other men. I could imagine him as comfortable helping fishermen as he would be accepting a gift from a patroness.

Those gathered around him shared his degree of comfort. It struck me that if this temple truly were a house of God instead of a monument to religious rule, this is how God might want his creatures to enjoy time in his presence.

This sanctuary of carefree enjoyment, however, ended as dozens of men entered the courtyard.

The delegation marched with the size, unison, and determination of a small army. Out of the thousands of priests who served at the temple, nearly fifty had been released from duty, and they formed the largest part of the wedge of men that approached Yeshua and his followers.

The priests wore long white gowns tied with girdles and white hats. Each had risen before dawn to take a ritual bath as part of his daily duties. The clash of a gong thrown onto the pavement in front of the temple had called the thousands to hours of ceremonial music and singing. Other priests had been scattered to perform the usual duties—offering sacrifices for pilgrims at the altar in front of the temple, lighting lamps, cleaning the altar of blood. These priests had been ordered to march here.

A much smaller group of elders and scribes—gathered from those who held places of honor among the highest tribunal of the Sanhedrin—led the priests. These men wore ordinary clothes that reflected their occupations, but the stiff dignity in their shoulders and faces clearly set them apart as men of power.

Finally, leading the delegation, Caiaphas set the pace. He, alone in the entire land, had the authority to wear the vestments of the high priest. On this occasion he had dressed to show his supreme position. A blue robe hung to his feet, covering his traditional white priestly garments except for the sleeves. The bottom of the robe had tassels with golden bells and pomegranates hung in alternation. Over the blue robe, he wore the ephod, a cape embroidered in bands of gold, purple, scarlet, and blue. A gold purse inset with twelve precious stones was attached to each shoulder of the ephod by gold broaches inset with sardonyxes. Caiaphas, a tall man already, had added to his height with a blue head-dress banded with gold.

The delegates had chosen the early hour with purpose; few pilgrims had gathered around the prophet yet to hear his teachings. The market in the Court of the Gentiles was nearly deserted by the merchants, for not many were brave enough to change money or sell livestock after the previous day's rebellion. In the relatively quiet temple, the audible padding of the priests' bare feet against the pavement made an ominous sound on their approach.

Dozens of men against a handful.

As the delegation neared, Peter was the only one to rise from the steps where Yeshua sat among the disciples. He stepped forward and waited, arms crossed, the hilt of his sword obvious from his girdle. However, at a few whispered words from Yeshua, Peter sat again.

When Caiaphas stopped, the delegation halted with him. He stared across a distance of twenty paces at the prophet from Nazareth. To any other Jew in the land, such a hostile glare from the highest religious authority would have been like a roar from God himself.

"Shalom," Yeshua said. "May God's peace rest upon you."

Caiaphas refused to answer. He had chosen to intimidate, to stand silent as the supreme judge. He nodded for one of the elders to move up beside him. They both stared at Yeshua.

"Shalom to you too," Yeshua said to the elder. "God has granted us a wonderful day in his presence."

"You have been teaching in the temple," the elder said. He was the same age as Caiaphas, almost as tall, but much heavier. He was completely bald, but his beard, streaked with gray and braided, touched his chest. "Do you deny this?"

Yeshua shook his head no.

"Let me be clear in front of all these witnesses," the elder said. "I am not suggesting you are a mere Haggadist, a teller of legends and stories. I am declaring that you actually teach. Do you deny this?"

Yeshua let a half smile touch his face. He understood. To the assembled priests and elders and scribes, this was a question of great importance.

Teaching followed a tradition, handed down from teacher to disciple, who, once granted authority, passed on the same information, unchanged. The most respected scholars were those who recited teachings word for word, nothing lost, nothing added. In any discussion, the ultimate appeal was always to an authority, whether a famous teacher or the Great Sanhedrin. Anyone who disagreed with the set authorities was seen as an ignorant scholar or a rebel to be banned.

"Do you deny that you teach?" the elder demanded again, his anger rising at the lack of fear on Yeshua's face.

Again, Yeshua shook his head no, acknowledging that yes, teaching had taken place.

Caiaphas, the imperious observer, smirked. The previous night's meeting in council had planned this perfectly, right down to the time the delegation would approach this peasant. Now, as calculated, the trap had been set. There was no way for the Nazarene to retreat.

"What authority do you have to do these things?" the elder asked. "Who gave you this authority?"

During the meeting, there had been a long, heated debate as the exact wording of the questions had been decided. It had to publicly appear that they were not merely challenging this man for his teachings; instead, they would be seen as following the duty that forced them to verify his background. After all, if Yeshua had done everything attributed to him, the elders had to protect the people by confirming these acts were not from Beelzebub, the devil who opposed God, did they not?

What authority do you have to do these things? Who gave you this authority? Caiaphas licked his lower lip, anticipating one of three answers. Unlikely as it was, the fool might actually answer Beelzebub, the devil, and the priests would have every right to take him to the temple wall and hurl him into the valley.

If he quoted a great Jewish teacher as his authority—the revered Hillel, for example—then the people would lose faith in him, for no Messiah would be lesser than another man.

The anticipation of a possible third answer, claiming authority from God, made Caiaphas's muscles twitch and tremble. Caiaphas had more than once engineered the immediate stoning of a rebel for heresy. And it would give him great pleasure to watch stones bite into the Nazarene peasant's flesh.

What authority do you have to do these things? Who gave you this authority? Yeshua had not yet replied. He turned his gaze from the elder to Caiaphas, as if he were reading the high priest's thoughts. For a missed heartbeat, Caiaphas felt the juice of fear wash against his stomach walls. Then he remembered the dozens of priests behind him and put the curl of scorn back onto his lips. In that moment, the hatred he held for the prophet's teachings became a personal hatred for the prophet.

"Will you not answer?" the elder demanded. "What authority do you have to do these things? Who gave you this authority?"

Yeshua leaned forward. Still sitting on the marble steps, he transferred his weight and leaned his elbows on the tops of his thighs.

"I will ask you one question," Yeshua replied. He began so casually, listeners not paying attention might have guessed this was simply another matter of teaching under discussion. "If you answer me, I will tell you what authority I have to do these things. Tell me: When John baptized people, was that authority from God or just from other people?"

Abruptly, Yeshua pushed himself up and stood.

"Tell me!" he commanded. His face, previously gentle and amused, had stiffened to match the sudden anger in his voice, as if an invisible mantle of power had been placed upon him, as if Yeshua were now judge and the delegation on trial.

Caiaphas actually took a half step back. He hated the peasant for it with a cold personal rage that he wanted to satisfy by plunging the sacrificial dagger into the man's liver.

"If we answer, 'John's baptism was from God,' Yeshua will say, 'Then why didn't you believe him?'" the elder whispered to Caiaphas in sudden panic.

Caiaphas did not answer. John the Baptist was believed by all to be a prophet sent directly from God. His stature was so great among the people that Caiaphas thought of John with envy and idly wondered at times if it might be worth it to be martyred.

"But if we say, 'It was from other people,' the crowd will be against us," the elder continued, his high whisper such a ridiculous squeak that the Galilee peasant and his disciples could most surely overhear it. Caiaphas, forearm muscles roped with the stress of his clenched hands, wanted to slap the elder for his indiscretion.

Caiaphas closed his eyes. With incredible will power, he held himself in a pose of indifference.

"I have duties at the altar," he finally said in a low voice to the elder. "You will remain and debate this among yourselves to keep him waiting. Then finally tell him that we don't know the answer to his question."

Caiaphas did not wait for the elder to affirm his order. The high priest turned with great dignity and walked through the delegation.

As he walked, he made his face a mask of peaceful contemplation. But thoughts of murder—savage murder with his own hands—heated his mind.

For Caiaphas could not fool himself.

The mountain had come to the prophet. The great ruling authority of hundreds of generations of religious tradition had challenged a solitary uneducated peasant carpenter. And lost.

Walking away was retreat.

As he left the courtyard, Caiaphas silently vowed to use all of his wealth, power, and cunning to end this peasant's life.

20

I spent another two hours watching. Waiting. The crowds around the prophet grew larger. My view of him was reduced to glimpses as he moved and spoke.

I watched his unfailing patience and cheerfulness. Laughter. Compassion. From those gathered around, I saw adoration. Awe. Skepticism. Occasional ridicule.

As entertainment, I could not think of a better way to spend my time.

And all the while, I let the seed of hope inside me take root and spread its branches. The reluctance I felt had gone. I no longer wondered *whether* I should approach him, but *how*.

Still, I was in no hurry.

But others were. . . .

Oren, son of Judd, nursed anger and a sore leg suffered in the chaos of the market the day before. He limped toward the residence of Caiaphas the high priest, protected from the direct heat of the sun by the walls lining the street. The noise and bustle of the lower city was long behind him. Here, in the enclave of the wealthy in upper Jerusalem overlooking the hectic confusion of the near slums below, little activity took place on the streets.

The palace of the high priest stood directly before him. Just inside the western wall that enclosed the city, it overlooked King David's tomb. It boasted an outer courtyard, an inner courtyard, a terraced garden, and dozens of luxurious rooms, including halls big enough to hold informal assemblies of the Sanhedrin.

The gates to each were guarded by servants who surveyed Oren's flushed, sweaty face with faintly hidden distaste as they listened to him wheeze his visit's purpose. And, at each gate, the servants hesitated unnecessarily before letting him through. As was the master, so were the servants—haughty and highly conscious of their stature.

Caiaphas met Oren in the garden. It was a clear indication of Oren's standing that he had not been invited into the palace.

"I know who you are," Caiaphas said, imperiously waving away Oren's introduction. "Let us not waste time."

The tall high priest stood in the shade of a fig tree.

"It is the market," Oren said. With the back of a fat, oily hand, he wiped sweat from his forehead. He had become acutely aware of his thirst, made deeper by the fact that Caiaphas had not sent a servant for refreshments. "The Nazarene has disrupted it completely."

"Your journey was wasted," Caiaphas said. "I know too well your complaint."

Oren's anger at the situation flared. He pulled up his tunic and twisted to point at the fat hairy calf of his right leg. The pasty flesh showed a deep purple bruise.

"Yesterday," Oren continued, "I was standing on my table to better see the confusion when an ox knocked it over and stepped on me. The commissions I send to you should be ample payment for protection."

"The peasant will be stopped," Caiaphas said. "Even now as we speak, he is being challenged."

"Like this morning?" Oren asked, happy for the chance to poke at the high priest's arrogance. "Word has spread wide that the entire ruling authority failed to move him from the temple courts. It has only increased his stature among the people. If this continues . . ."

Oren was rewarded with a clenched smile from Caiaphas.

"It will not," the high priest hissed. "Even as you and I speak, a new trap is about to be sprung."

21

I continued to stand patiently among the crowd, leaning against a pillar at the side of the court, content to listen to the on-going discussions. I did not bother to strain to look over the crowd at the man named Yeshua.

The voices carried to me clearly; like me, none of the spectators engaged in idle conversation, and any noise from the crowd came in whispered reactions to points of debate, then stopped as all waited to hear the counterpoint.

Occasionally, however, I did stand on the tips of my toes to see if any of the scene had changed. At first glance, the contest seemed overwhelmingly unfair.

On one side, lawyers and scribes—white-bearded, white-clothed Pharisees armed with scrolls; Sadducees dressed with the wealth that comes with success in politics; fresh-faced students in black robes, eager for the chance to show their verbal skills. Jerusalem's intellectual elite had gathered in full force.

Facing them, alone, was the carpenter from Nazareth. As if his unassuming clothing did not give enough indication of his lack of status, every word he spoke in his rough Galilean accent reminded the audience of his lack of education.

". . . surely you have read this in the Scriptures," Yeshua continued, "'The stone that the builders rejected became the cornerstone.'"

"Yes, yes," one of the students called, "from the Book of Psalms. By excellent use of a pun, the author implies that the cornerstone is also a leader. As part of a victory celebration, the author undoubtedly meant to exhort the people to song."

The student smiled at the crowd, proud of his feat of immediate recall.

Another spoke to Yeshua in the thrusting manner of debate the pack of intellectuals had been using. "It is only a fragment of Scripture. What does this have to do with a tale about the tenants of a vineyard who kill the landowner's son when he arrives to collect the grapes?"

"The kingdom of God will be taken away from you," Yeshua replied, "and given to people who do the things God wants in his kingdom."

"No!" one of the white-bearded men shouted, his voice surprisingly powerful. "No! You cannot speak to us like that!"

Yeshua raised his eyebrows as reply. It brought laughter from the crowd, for few of the poorer pilgrims missed the implications. These Pharisees and the rest of the elite felt Yeshua was speaking directly to them as the tenants who rejected the son; their guilty consciences had been pricked to immediate anger.

Some of the older Pharisees turned away, seething with frustrated rage, grumbling for the man's arrest.

Everyone else in the crowd stayed, however. Never before had one of them—one of the lowly—tweaked the ears of the high and mighty.

Yeshua turned to answer some questions quietly, and the

rest of the crowd began to talk in low tones, marveling at Yeshua's poise.

It was during this pause in public debate that I stepped forward.

I had chosen to speak with the red-bearded man named Peter. His wide, young face made him appear approachable despite his scowl. From his simple clothing, I assumed he would be easily impressed. And the fact that he kept his hand on the hilt of a half-hidden sword showed me he was the one who watched guard. He, then, was the one who could get me into the inner circle.

Peter was at the edge of the crowd surrounding Yeshua. I moved closer to him, greeting him with, "Shalom."

His eyes narrowed as he appraised my expensive clothing and neatly trimmed beard and hair. I hoped he would see what all others did in dealings with me: a man of even features despite my scar, tall enough to be imposing, with a smile to offset any intimidation rendered by my size.

"Are you another of the Pharisee spies?" he asked. "Testing to see if I tire of following the teacher?"

"No," I said.

"You dress like one of them."

I removed my cloak and set it on the shoulders of a beggar near me. He turned to me in surprise, and I waved him on, indicating that he could keep the cloak.

"No longer," I said.

"What do you want?" Whatever sympathy I might have gained was offset by his suspicion of my generous gesture. The cloak was worth a month's wages for a laborer.

"An audience with your master," I said.

"But he makes time for everybody."

Why was this man impatient with me? Usually the lesser privileged treated me with deferential respect.

"I wish to see him privately," I said.

Peter pulled his own cloak back to further expose the hilt of his sword.

"How do I know this is not a trap?" he demanded. "Men like you want him captured. It is a simple matter to pretend you need healing."

"No," I said quickly. This was not going as I intended. "I mean him no harm. I merely wish to speak with him . . . to ask him something."

Peter stared at me, yielding no ground.

I felt the stirring of desperation. Without servants around me to establish my importance, I was failing quickly in my efforts to impress this man.

"It's my daughter," I said. "She . . . she . . ."

I drew a breath. "She needs help. I have nowhere else to turn."

The sun-beaten wrinkles around Peter's eyes softened. His hand fell away from the hilt of his sword.

His obvious sympathy came as such a relief that I pressed on. Stupidly.

"I have gold," I said. "Tell him I will give generously to his cause. Whatever price he names."

Had I slapped the man, the change in him could not have happened faster.

"The teacher cannot be bought." Peter's shoulders tightened. His face became a mask again. "Take your gold elsewhere."

"But my daughter . . ."

"Go," Peter said. "If you offer payment, it is obvious you do not understand."

"But—"

Peter put his hand on my shoulder, ready to push me away. Before we could argue further, something compelled me to turn toward the prophet. The crowd had parted slightly, and I saw that he was looking directly at us.

Peter had also turned to look. He caught his master's gaze and dropped his hand.

Again, I was held by those eyes. Compassionate. Gentle. Eyes that drew me forward. I even took a step toward him but was stopped by sudden muttering from within the crowd.

Important-looking men had begun to push their way through the crowd.

"Herodians," someone near me whispered. "I have seen them arguing politics in the plaza."

"With Pharisees?" another asked. "What has brought them together?"

22

*H*erodians. A political party, determined to see Herod rather than a Roman governor rule. They were hated by the religious authorities who knew that Herod would strip them of their power at his first chance.

Their politics were in direct conflict with the Sanhedrin, who, much as they despised Roman rule, despised Herod more. After all, his tyrannical father, Herod the Great, had not only replaced the high priests at whim but had also murdered many of the great sages who dared protest his acts.

Herodians joined with Pharisees. The cause that had brought them together, I knew, would prove interesting.

I stepped back again, not wishing the attention that would fall on me if I persisted in trying to reach Yeshua at this moment.

Once again at the back of the crowd, leaning against my comforting pillar, I noticed something that did not bode well for Yeshua.

Temple police—discretely waiting among the columns at the rear of the courtyard.

The Pharisees Elidad and Gaal—both handsome elderly men with the dignity of fully white beards—expected it to be their finest public moment. Even so, Elidad's legs trembled, and he hoped his tunic hid the movement. Gaal stood with his chest puffed, secure in the knowledge that they had been sent by Caiaphas, who had assured them that the peasant would recognize neither of them. So certain were they of success, they had brought along temple guards.

Each man made a great show of bowing in respect to Yeshua. When he acknowledged them, Elidad began, speaking with the greatest sincerity he could muster. "Teacher, we know that you are an honest man and that you teach the truth about God's way."

Yeshua had a habit of cocking one eyebrow in an expression of gentle inquisitiveness. His face was set thus as he waited for the men to continue.

"Yes," Gaal said, with his hands stretched and open in welcoming friendliness as he had practiced, "you are not afraid of what other people think about you because you pay no attention to who they are."

At that precise moment, a flock of pigeons passed overhead, their shadows rushing away like disappearing fish. One, however, left more behind than the quick dappled movement of shade across pavement; it had deposited a large sticky pellet of white directly into the center of Gaal's open right hand. He closed his fingers over his palm quickly, hoping no one in the crowd had noticed, for if anyone drew a symbolic conclusion about the pigeon's judgment of their speech, the laughter would never cease.

"So tell us," Elidad said to Yeshua, unaware of what had happened to his partner, "what you think."

Elidad, as planned, let a dramatic pause hang as a prelude to his question, one that would end the peasant's teachings.

As Gaal felt the discomfort of the messy liquid seeping between his fingers, it crossed his mind that if Yeshua was the Messiah and capable of raising the dead, perhaps the pigeon's gift had not been coincidence. Worse, it seemed Yeshua was enjoying a secret smile as he surveyed them both during Elidad's dramatic pause.

"Is it right," Elidad resumed, "to pay taxes to Caesar or not?"

Silence. To Gaal, it was a wonderful silence, one that more than made up for the indignity of the pigeon's droppings. Silence. The crowd was not whispering or laughing or cheering the prophet. Everyone understood the importance of his answer. No true Messiah would acknowledge an earthly power. Answering yes, then, would destroy his power among the people.

Yet if he answered no to keep his popularity with the masses, he would immediately be taken away and charged with sedition, for the Roman authorities only tolerated local religions to a certain extent.

Nor could he decline to answer, not if he wanted to keep his reputation.

The silence lengthened. The question, in its cunning, was masterful.

Yeshua stood and moved toward the two Pharisees. When he finally spoke, he began so softly that all had to strain to hear him.

"You hypocrites!" he said, all humor gone from his face. "Why are you trying to trap me?"

Facing the full power of the man's character, neither Elidad nor Gaal could stammer a reply.

"Show me a coin used for paying the tax," Yeshua ordered.

Elidad patted his pockets. Gaal remained frozen with fear and the discomfort of his soiled right hand.

Elidad finally found a denarius. He reached across the short distance and handed it to Yeshua.

"Whose image and name are on the coin?" Yeshua asked them both, loudly enough for the crowd and all the intellectual elite to hear.

"Caesar's," they both said quickly, feeling like delinquent children under full inspection.

Yeshua turned. He gathered the hems of his robe, walked back to the steps, and with great dignity, seated himself again. His deliberate slow movements further chastised Elidad and Gaal, as it left them alone before the crowd, the center of attention.

When ready, Yeshua flipped the small coin back toward Gaal, who tried to grab it with his left hand and feebly missed. The light clink of the coin on pavement was obvious testimony to the incompetence he felt in front of the teacher.

"Give to Caesar the things that are Caesar's," Yeshua said, "and give to God the things that are God's."

Their stunned silence settled like a cloak of total defeat.

23

In the tumult of amazement and laughter that followed Yeshua's deft answer to a seemingly impossible question, he took opportunity to refresh himself with food and drink, served by women from the crowd.

I did not blame him. As it was, his stamina impressed me greatly. He had spoken publicly for several hours; from the few political dealings I had had, I understood fully the strain and exhaustion of concentrating intensely under such pressure.

Later, when Yeshua began to speak again, it was in parables—short, interesting stories that held simple, yet powerful messages. The bulk of his audience were uneducated peasants. It was easy to see why they preferred his teachings over the dry, scholarly, legalistic lectures of the Pharisees.

I, too, enjoyed listening but not without a degree of restlessness. I greatly wished to speak to the man alone but saw no good opportunity.

Worse, when he had finished his teachings, he retreated with his followers to another courtyard, requesting some time of privacy after promising to speak again in a few hours.

I stayed back, like all the crowd, out of respect. But I did not fall too far back. During our short few seconds of contact, his eyes had spoken to me. I was determined to get my audience.

So I trailed Yeshua and his followers from an appropriate distance.

As they rested on the steps in the Court of Women, I saw as he pointed over the hundreds of people milling about.

I was too far away to hear his words, of course. Much later, after all the bad and good that happened, I learned what had caused him to stop and draw attention to an elderly woman who walked slowly, apart from the crowds.

No one, not even his followers, ever spoke to her then or later, so I admit to speculation in trying to describe the courtyard through her eyes. . . .

The old woman had inexplicably become uncertain of her name. At times, she wept with frustration, trying to recall it. Other times, especially at night with the chill of the street pressing into her cold bones, she listened for the sound of it, certain that somewhere in her life others had spoken it to her. As she strained to hear it, fragmented memories of people once important to her flickered through her awareness like ghosts in a dark chamber. When she clutched at their hems to beg for conversation, the ghosts became smoke in her fingers, leaving behind a sadness and sense of loss all the more overwhelming because she had no memories to structure her grief.

To the people in the temple court, who moved around her slow, unsteady progress like water streaming past a worn boulder, her stricken efforts to find her identity were mumbled incantations from a living skull pasted with thin white hair. To them, she was insignificant—bowed, shrunken, trembling flesh wrapped in filthy rags.

It was Passover. Despite the disease that had eroded her mind, the old woman understood that. An instinct drew her to the Court of Women and the thirteen trumpet-shaped boxes beneath the roofed pillars. Perhaps deep in the mysteries of her mind, a framework set by her years of dwelling with her husband and children and her faithful devotion to Yahweh still served her. Or perhaps, shorn of every worldly distraction, her spirit had emerged in a triumph of sorts, freely seeking its Creator before her life force left her old body, and in so doing providing the woman the only glow of joy she could carry until her last breath left her chest.

She did not remember her name.

But she knew the shards of round metal biting into the flesh of her palm had value. Had any of the passersby forced open her hand, they would have torn from her two perutahs, which added together were only a ninety-sixth of a denarius, all that she could expect to earn in a day of labor, and by law, the least any person could contribute to the temple coffers as sacrifice.

With her head down, she shuffled, confused, toward the treasury boxes, a solitary figure in the vastness of the temple courts.

The self-righteous, armed with gold and silver, ready to demand God's presence, passed by her without a glance. The cheerful, thinking not of the tithes they were about to drop, but of families and meals waiting as soon as they finished their temple duty, also passed by her. Children passed by. Women lost in thoughts of love passed by. Priests, afraid to defile themselves by any contact with a female, passed her.

And slowly, unaware of Yeshua's presence, she passed him where he rested against a pillar.

She remained unaware of him as she dropped the coins into the treasury, unaware as she prayed before the rising incense of her sacrifice, and unaware as she turned to retrace the long painful journey to the streets where she would sleep the night. She was unaware that he turned to his disciples and told them that her gift, which had reached his Father, was far beyond any wealth on earth.

As she neared the peasant man, however, something beckoned her spirit. The woman rarely lifted her head—it was a habit she had developed in the days when she'd had enough comprehension to feel her humiliation, when she'd realized it was easier not to see pity or scorn in the eyes of those who noticed her.

She heard the call to her soul, however, as strong as the light from the sun. His call overcame her years of habit, and she stopped, balancing on her cane as she peered through her milky white eyes almost completely filmed with cataracts.

Unself-consciously, she met the man's gaze.

Sunshine flooded the dark sad chambers of her memory.

With her head lifted, she saw not the man named Yeshua, rather she saw flashes of images—the tall dark handsomeness of the man she'd married, and their girl-child at her breast, and a reflection of herself in a mirror when her flesh was smooth and her smile not vacant.

Yeshua did not speak to her. She did not speak to him. She did not know he was a prophet. Or that many followed him. Or that, as young and strong as he was, he would find death before she did.

People stepped between them, and she moved on.

Only now, joy gave her new strength.

The light that had returned her memories had given her one more thing.

She remembered her name.

24

I did not have another chance to approach the prophet until early evening. He had spent the afternoon teaching, again in parables, denouncing the religious orders, making prophecies.

Everything about him fascinated me. I allowed my hope to grow stronger. I stayed on the fringes of those around him. Invisible. Quiet. Watching. Waiting.

And, as many of the pilgrims departed from the temple, I saw my opportunity. Some Greeks had asked him to explain his teachings, and when he finished, I was able to move close.

He greeted me with a smile.

The evening shadows had begun to fall, and the light was soft on his face.

Because so many people had been pulling at him all day, I felt I needed to keep my time with him short.

"I am here for Passover," I said quickly. "I have left behind my wife and daughter."

His beautiful smile did not waver.

"My daughter suffers," I continued. "Everything that I have, I would willingly trade for her to be healed."

"Understand who I am," Yeshua replied. He spoke so softly that no one overheard us. "Then return to me."

"Please," I said. "She is horribly scarred. There was . . ."

I debated with myself, then decided my burden did not matter. Only hers.

"There was a fire," I said. "Started by a lamp. The oil spilled on her legs, and she was trapped in the flames. She lies in bed, unable to move. She cries constantly from the pain. Please, let me pay for your journey. Come to my town. Or wait until I bring her to you. Heal her. Every possession I have earned I will give to you and your cause."

If only he could see what I saw every day. When the sound of laughter reached her from children playing in the street, she bowed her head in defeat. The slowly healing skin—mottled and rough like a toad's back—had tightened, bending her legs like bows, forming a web behind her knees. Some days, even the light pressure of a blanket on her legs raised shrieks of agony. I doubted my once beautiful daughter would ever draw another breath without pain, and there were days when I wondered if she might be better off in the release of death.

Surely, if Yeshua saw her, he would have compassion on her. Others turned away from my once beautiful daughter in horror at her agony, but this man, I knew, would reach out to her.

"You would give all your possessions?" he asked. Again, softly.

"Yes," I said without hesitation. I could always earn them back again. What did a few years of poverty matter against the possibility of redemption? Hers. Mine.

"Thus it would be your doing that heals her?"

The disciples had begun to move close to us. I could see they were ready to send me away from him.

"My doing?" I answered in confusion. "I don't understand. You have the healing touch. I've seen it. Other cripples have walked at your command. Surely you can restore my daughter's legs. You can take away the pain that prevents her from sleeping. You can—"

"Understand who I am before you ask. Understand how you have chosen to ask—and why it is wrong. Then return to me."

He rejoined his disciples. In the growing darkness, I could not read the expression on his face. Was it disappointment? Sorrow?

I recognized that I had been dismissed. Many times I, too, had dismissed others. I knew it would be futile to chase after him.

I watched the prophet from Galilee walk away.

As my hope disappeared, anger began to fill the hole it left behind.

25

I am told you spent much of the day following the rebel prophet," Pascal said without any preliminary small talk.

We sat together in a small private courtyard within his mansion. The day's heat had passed, and evening shadows darkened the flowers on the shrubs that surrounded us. Except for the matters to be discussed, it would have been a pleasant place to idle the time before our meal with Seraphine.

"You have spies who watch my every movement?" I said it mildly, but we both knew I was angry.

"No," he answered. "But you must admit that your scar makes you an easy figure to notice. I am not unknown among the Sadducees at the temple, and many people know you are my guest. In this city, most gossip of any importance reaches me."

"I will not deny my presence in the temple," I said. "I would not, however, call myself a follower."

"What you are is much different—and from my viewpoint, less important—than what people perceive you to be." He also spoke mildly, but I felt his anger. "I warned you last evening of this danger."

I shrugged. My pretended indifference was a mistake.

He leaned forward, no longer concealing his anger. "You and I have arranged to sit here to discuss the purchase of your holdings. But first you must understand that already some of my customers, the wealthy and elite of Jerusalem, have threatened to cancel orders because of my association with you."

"What is more important?" I asked, feeling my blood heat too. "Family and friendship? Or customers?"

"I could ask you the same thing. We carry the same blood, and we have been friends for years. But when I asked you to stay away from a foolish rebel, you chose him over me."

"I have not chosen him!"

"That is irrelevant. To all of Jerusalem—"

"Hardly. You speak of a handful of stiff-necked, arrogant men who think the world should bow to them."

Pascal's voice tightened. "The world does bow to them. At least the world in which we live. If they *think* you are a follower, then to them you *are* a follower. And that hurts me. So my point carries. You have chosen him over me."

He glared at me. "In practical terms, it is also an unintelligent decision. This lone peasant of yours has angered the entire spectrum of established religious and political parties."

Pascal gestured wide with both hands. "It's remarkable, actually. He has done the impossible and managed to unite them. Usually when one group wants something, the other will block it, just for spite. This prophet's success, however, means it serves everyone's best interests to see him dead."

"Dead?"

"All you have to do is listen to how you and I have just argued. He provokes severe reactions."

"But dead?" If the miracles were truly miracles, if he was truly the Messiah, surely he had the power to save his own life.

"Simeon, you have lost your hard edge, your ability to assess any new situation. How can you expect to thrive among the other keen businessmen when you fail to read the political winds?"

Pascal's chastisement was accurate and deserved. I didn't defend myself, but listened as he continued.

"It's simple," Pascal said. "The Herodians see that as Yeshua assumes more earthly authority, Herod has less chance of gaining control of Judea. As for the Pharisees, he not only insults them publicly, but he also outright contradicts them and has gained such a following that people may actually leave the synagogues, especially with all this talk about the long-awaited Messiah. The Sadducees? He has disrupted their lucrative income from the temple markets; it is clear he is a threat to more than their religious beliefs."

"But killing him," I protested. "That's murder."

"All they need to do is get him before the Sanhedrin. The trial won't be fair, but that doesn't matter. The powerful elite want him dead. And so he will die. You of all people should know that is the way of the world."

Pascal softened, opening his arms to welcome me as he had upon my arrival. "Simeon, let us not argue over this man."

I let him believe my silence was agreement.

"I think I understand why you want me to purchase your ships and warehouses and shops," he said quietly. "And I will if you insist because in the long run, it will make me a considerably richer man. But I am begging you to reconsider and go home. If in six months you still feel the same, return to Jerusalem and we will discuss it seriously."

"You mean in six months your friends will have forgotten that I listened to a rebel's words." I *was* bitter.

"You are unkind. I am concerned about you." He hesitated, searched his mind for a way to continue, drew a deep breath, pushed on. "If you can forgive me for saying this, as one friend who cares for another, I am afraid grief is pushing you to a rash decision."

"Yes," I said, careful not to reject his sympathy, despite my irritation with him. "I do grieve."

Again it flashed through my mind. The screams, the flames, the blackened walls falling in, the confusion of the smoke, the searing heat, the agony of my face, my daughter's burned flesh. Pascal could never understand.

"Listen to me, cousin," I said. "Nothing will change my mind. I intend to give you a list of what I believe my estate is worth. I request you pay me only half the value. Once you agree, I will leave you instructions on how to make payment."

"*Leave* me instructions? Are you going somewhere?"

"I am sorry," I said. "What I meant to say was that I will *give* you instructions."

He stared at me. I returned his stare.

I needed to become a better liar.

The evening meal I shared with Pascal and Seraphine was muted by my low mood. All I had ahead of me was a long, sleepless night, an ordeal whose difficulty would in no way be diminished because of my familiarity with the dark hours of remorse and sorrow.

In another part of the city, a small drama was about to begin. I later learned of it from the servant girl who stood outside the door and listened to every word. . . .

26

Oil lamps set every few paces gave uneven light to the long corridor in the palace of the high priest. An elderly man, robed in purple, walked vigorously behind a maidservant, aware of her youth and freshness. When she reached a door at the end of the corridor, she stopped and bowed.

The elderly man smiled a snake's smile above his neatly trimmed beard. He smoothed back thick gray hair, showing off the wide gold bands on his fingers.

"He awaits you here," the maid said, hiding her instinctive revulsion behind cold politeness.

"Go then," he said, not the least disappointed. For every maid put off by his advanced years, there were two others who saw past his wrinkled skin and understood the warmth and vigor of gold and jewels.

She stepped away, and he pushed the door open.

Inside, more oil lamps flickered, illuminating the tile floor covered with luxurious carpet, the furniture made of oiled cedar, and bronze statues brought from Greece. A man stood at the far end of the room, looking through a window that offered a magnificent view of the darkened buildings of the lower city.

The old man shut the door.

"Yes, my son, you sent for me?" he asked.

Caiaphas turned from his thoughts at the window. He frowned at the amused solicitous tone of the elderly man's voice.

"Don't posture with me," Caiaphas said sourly. "This is far from a public gathering where the great and hallowed Annas must preserve the pious sanctimony of a former high priest."

"A son-in-law must show more respect," Annas said. His laughter sounded like wind shaking dry husks. "Regardless of the irritations of office."

"That is easy for you to say. With respect and wealth and connections, you have all the advantages of holding office and none of the grief."

Annas reached for a jug of wine and poured himself some. He took a long drink before answering. "Why do you think I appointed one son after the other and finally turned to you? It is far better to have *been* a high priest than to *be* one. Especially with the current situation at the temple."

He took more wine, then smiled his snake smile at Caiaphas. "Which, I presume, is why I am here."

Caiaphas began to pace. "Without the temple market, have you any idea how much revenue we have lost in the last two days?"

"Of course," Annas said, still amused. He set the wine goblet down. "Years ago I supervised the delicate negotiations for the 'commissions' to our family coffers."

"If the prophet is not dealt with soon," Caiaphas hissed, "your delicate structure will never rise again. If the people see the temple can exist without the market, they'll never let us begin again."

"Well, well. The prophet has destroyed your profit."

Annas chuckled at his play on words. "And you led us to believe that it was for the safety of our country he must die, not because of money." Annas tapped his chin theatrically as he mused.

"Ah yes," he said moments later, "wasn't it in front of the entire Sanhedrin that you declared it better for one man to die than for a whole nation to perish?"

"Politics and convenience do not lessen a truth," Caiaphas answered. "Even Joseph of Arimathea and Nicodemus remain silent, understanding the peasant must not be allowed to bring this country to rebellion."

"More wine? From the heat in your voice it sounds like you have already indulged—despite the ritual purification necessary for an acting high priest."

"You are attempting to provoke me further. I know your nature. You stir with a stick and see what rises. Some day you will uncover a nest of bees, and then I shall laugh at you the way you laugh at me."

Annas walked to the window and faced away from Caiaphas as he spoke. "I am amused because I believe this is the first time I have seen emotion from you. Not even when you married my daughter did I detect any flow of blood."

"The man must die."

"Even in the face of the miracles he has wrought within the temple these last few days?"

Caiaphas snorted. "He is nothing more than a magician, hiring people to walk in lame and run out leaping."

Annas turned back from the window. For the first time since entering the room, his voice lost its banter. "I have made queries about some of those people. Neighbors swear they have been lame or blind from birth. I am not so certain it is fraud. This man intrigues me. Someday, I would like time alone with him."

Caiaphas stopped pacing. "If he is not a magician, then he is from the devil."

"You *do* want him dead."

"You weren't there when he publicly denounced us."

Caiaphas had to lean against a nearby table to keep his hands from shaking with rage. "'Whitewashed tombs,' he called us. Beautiful on the outside yet full of dead men's bones."

Annas shrugged. "The poor always vilify the rich. I learned long ago that wealth is a wonderful balm against insults."

"Insults? He called into question our integrity, our teachings, our authority. You were not there to see the people cheer his words. This man must die!"

Caiaphas swept his arm across the table, sending the wine jug and goblets smashing against the wall.

"You have gone far past amusement," Annas said in the resulting silence. "There is great danger in passionate action not grounded in cold thought. If your foolish rage threatens everything I have built . . ."

Had Caiaphas not been so flushed with the joy of hatred, he would have quailed; only rarely did Annas showed the steel of his absolute rule.

"I shall have both his death and my satisfaction!" Caiaphas continued, riding the wave of his emotion. "Here, in this very room, will I send him to his knees!"

Annas stepped toward Caiaphas. He reached up and grabbed the younger man's angular chin and squeezed until Caiaphas was ready to listen.

"Do not act in haste," Annas said in a soft voice. "If you take him publicly, there will be a riot. That could very well spark the people to the rebellion you fear if you let him live."

Annas continued to squeeze until all resistance had left his son-in-law. "Do you understand?"

"We will take him in private," Caiaphas said, almost dizzy with his hatred. First the humiliation in the temple court. Now this humiliation with Annas.

Annas dropped his hand. "How? Have you thought this through? It is difficult to track his whereabouts. He comes and goes at will."

"One of his followers could solve that difficulty," Caiaphas answered. "Over the past days, I have sent spies out to test his disciples one by one. Not in such a way to raise their suspicions, but simply to discover any disloyalty."

"And?" Annas asked.

"Eleven of the twelve are as resolute as stone—so totally worshipful that they either did not comprehend the subtlety of my spies or turned their backs and walked away."

"I take it you are suggesting one might be persuaded to betray him."

"Yes, there is a possibility," Caiaphas said. "He is a poor man, his father sent to debtor's prison. Vaguely effeminate and obviously lustful for power. We can appeal to that and make him feel important."

Caiaphas pressed his fingers together and smiled. "His name is Judas."

WEDNESDAY

27

My dearest love,

Remember our days of innocence? The first few years after our wedding? If only I could find a way back to those easy hours of reclining with my head in your lap as you stroked my hair. We happily traded stories of our childhood, laughed, joked, and hummed silly melodies. Oh the wonders of love with you, the joyful mystery of abandon in each other's arms, the drowsy smiles as we woke together, the way the bumps rose on your skin when I lightly ran my fingernails across your arms, your shoulders, your back.

If, somehow, I could find my way back to you, I would pledge myself again. This time, knowing the dangers that destroy love, I would guard against the gradual selfishness that eroded what we had. I would be a man you could trust and love. Never again would I neglect the small touches and smiles that I now know matter more than the wealth that supplies the clatter of servants in a large, empty house.

Oh, that I could be with you again.

Yesterday, I woke with the hope that I would be able to return to you, to start over.

Today, I wake with disappointment. The man I approached to heal Vashti sent me away, and did so in a manner that neither confirmed nor denied he could help her.

My disappointment is all the more bitter against the hope I had allowed myself. I was a fool for entertaining the ridiculous idea that anyone could take away our daughter's pain and make her whole again. As this day begins, after hours of reflection through the night, I see I was a fool, too, for approaching a crazed man with that hope.

When a man believes in me, I heard this man say yesterday in the temple, he does not believe in me only, but also in the One who sent me.

When a man looks at me, I heard him say, he sees the One who sent me.

I have come into the world as a light, I heard him say, so that no one who believes in me should stay in darkness.

My love, can you see me waving my arms in exasperation as I tell you this? (Remember the days when I was eager to share with you all the happenings in my daily life, and you laughed at me for how my arms moved as I spoke?)

My love, what kind of man tells others to believe in him? As if he is a god. Or the God—I have heard rumors that he so claims.

Only an insane man would declare this. Not a great teacher as some call him, but an insane man.

Yet . . .

I did see him perform miracles.

It seems to me that everything rests on that. If the miracles are real, my rational mind can accept the premise that he is more than man. And at the same time, my rational mind cannot accept the premise of God among us as a lowly peasant.

My mind circles and circles.

(Here I am, thinking aloud in your presence, as I did in the days before silence settled on us like a frost, unaware it was there until far too much of the cold had arrived.)

The evidence of my eyes and ears tells me it is preposterous to believe that the world is moved by an invisible hand; preposterous to believe that if such a spirit does exist, it has chosen to reside in the body of a man; preposterous to think that this man Yeshua could turn water into wine, stop a storm with his voice, or raise a man from the dead.

Yet . . .

During the long sleepless hours last night, I realized it is equally preposterous to contemplate a world that is not moved by an invisible hand. My flesh and blood and bones come from the very soil of this earth, nourished by bread made of wheat that draws from moisture and sunlight and soil, strengthened by the meat of animals that feed upon those plants, sustained by the water that falls from the skies and collects in rivers and lakes.

My body gurgles and groans, and somehow, despite the vulgarity of decay that comes with this flesh, there is something unseen in me that fills with love or hate or greed or compassion—and remorse and regret, which weigh so heavily that I tire of life.

That the world exists, and that I exist in the world is a great mystery itself, dulled only because I see and live it everyday without giving it thought.

Thus, I am forced to admit it is a preposterous notion to believe our world exists without the unseen hand of a Creator. If then there is a Creator who breathes spirit into me, could he not have the power to choose to become flesh himself?

So my mind circles. One is as preposterous as the other. God cannot be. Or we cannot be without God.

How am I to know? And why, after all these years of comfortable life, am I suddenly tormented with these questions?

It is this man Yeshua. His message and his deeds confront me.

I tell myself he is a lunatic.

Yet . . .

As he spoke yesterday in the temple, indeed in the moment he finished declaring glory to God, a loud noise split the skies. Some said it was thunder, but the sky was cloudless. Others fell to their knees, believing they heard angels. Still others in the temple declared it was the voice of God.

Miracles, the voice of God . . . Yeshua is a man impossible to ignore.

God or man?

I cannot rest until I know. Against all rational thought, in the depths of my disappointment, there remains in my heart a small ember of hope. I am in desperate need, stuck in the darkness of this deep hole I have fallen into. If he is light . . .

God or man?

Today I will seek him.

God or man?

That is what I must decide before I write any final farewell to you.

28

I waited but did not find him. I spent hours in the temple, sitting on the steps among the columns of the Outer Court, made more miserable by a gloomy cloud that passed over and dropped a light rain. Neither the gloom nor drizzle slowed the hectic activities of pilgrims and priests around me; men and women bustled in all directions, with obvious purpose.

As for me, I did nothing. I was waiting for redemption.

As the long minutes passed, my heart became heavier. Why, I wondered, did nothing in this temple promise me relief from the one single action that had cost me so much?

I knew I owed the truth to my wife before I died, and I hoped there would be a small measure of relief in lancing that heavy boil of conscience. But as I watched the activities of the temple, I could not imagine finding consolation in approaching a somber priest garbed in white robes to confess what I had done. I had already judged myself; I did not need another's stares of superiority to confirm the vileness that shrouded me.

Nor, despite my proximity to the temple altar, did I believe I could find forgiveness by brutally taking the life of a creature as much unaware of my sins as of its impending death; no amount of innocent blood could wash me clean.

I knew this because I had tried with repeated sacrifices.

A Gentile might recoil from this brutality, thinking the sacrifice of an animal's life was meant as a gift to appease God.

Not so. Our Hebrew word for sacrifice—*korban*—comes from the same root that means "to approach." Those who believe in a living God see man as living between the spiritual and physical worlds. Caught between a battle of the darker desires of flesh and the imprisoned soul's desire to reach God, man constantly struggles to overcome this contradiction. In bringing *korban,* the death offering serves not as appeasement, but as the demonstration of what man would deserve were God to judge him.

Thus—and it is difficult for scoffing Gentiles to accept this subtlety—the God of creation is not an unforgiving ogre who demands the final thrashings of an animal as a substitute for punishment. Instead, we are taught that he is a God of love who offered Jews this sacrificial system as a way of restoring spiritual life. For the sacrifice, if offered with true repentance, represents the death of the man's physical nature, freeing him to bring his true self into connection with God, elevating him by temporarily giving his spiritual nature victory over his physical.

But months of weekly sacrifices had not redeemed me.

Yes, I was filled with repentance, with remorse beyond self-hatred.

And yes, a lamb's blood allowed me *korban,* to approach. But God, I had decided, would not listen to me, no matter how closely I approached.

I was also miserably conscious that, for what I had done, any creature's death was too little a price to pay.

I could buy hundreds more sheep and spill enough blood to

overflow the cracks of the stone floor. Yet that river of life would merely cost me more of my surplus of gold. Where was my punishment in that?

Sitting, waiting, dwelling on all of this, it simply became clearer that only one death would suffice.

Mine. Unless I found a miracle.

And the rain fell harder.

29

I was destined not to find the prophet, for as I would learn before the day ended, this, the day before Passover, was a day on which he rested near Bethany in seclusion.

Where Yeshua had peace, another, like me, had a horribly restless soul, though for different reasons from mine.

The other was named Judas.

He probably passed almost within my reach among the crowd as he hurried to find the high priests. There is only a field of blood to speak for him now, and I cannot pretend to know his heart and what sent him into Jerusalem.

Still, for me, speculation is inevitable, as it probably is for any who later heard of his secret visit to the temple. . . .

In the gloominess on the Mount of Olives, donkeys brayed at the city gates across the valley. Singing and chanting came from behind the temple walls. But none of these sounds broke into Judas's mind.

During a poor night's sleep, he had spent his wakeful times alternating between vindictive satisfaction as he thought of his revenge against the slights he had endured and renewed lapses of guilt as he realized the path his vengeful thoughts took him.

Now, they took him on a literal path, down the Mount of Olives. Jerusalem drew him like a siren of the Greek myths, beckoning him not with promises of the flesh, but with the much sweeter prospect of power among the city's elite—power that Yeshua had chosen to discard, and in so doing, had wasted three years of Judas's life.

Not just three years, Judas thought, but everything he had held dear before meeting Yeshua.

Outside his Judean hometown, his brother now tended the small herd of goats Judas had built from a sickly pregnant nanny over the course of ten seasons. Why? Because in a moment marked as clearly as a watershed on the nearby ravines, Judas remembered the messianic impulse that had swept him to run home and sell those goats for a mere note of promise; as part of a crowd, he'd watched the teacher send a lame man dancing away in joy. All his life, Judas had used aggressive hard work to bury the shame of watching his father go a debtor's prison for gambling. All his life, Judas had lusted for the security and respectability of wealth, seething at the injustice of belonging to the poor while men of lesser intelligence and character strutted in mastery. Yet on that incredible afternoon, when the teacher's glance had fallen upon him, the gaze had felt like hot water scathing dirt off crusted old leather. The teacher, Judas had known without doubt in that moment, understood the filth of the meanness of spirit that had been forced upon him and, in that depth of complete understanding, had also accepted Judas without reservation.

From that one watershed moment, Judas had worked hard—with the same flailing, scrabbling ambition he had applied to growing his goat herd—to gain his position among the followers the teacher most trusted. The teacher had even appointed him among only twelve to preach and drive out demons and take the teachings to the people.

More and more, however, Judas had begun to feel like the shamed outsider he had been as a teenager, jeered by the village boys. A Judean among close-knit Galileans. A slender man among broad-shouldered fishermen with tough hands scarred by years of handling heavy wet netting.

Judas could mark that first moment of isolation, too—the moment when the teacher had first thrown a shadow over Judas's hopes. Word had come that John the Baptist had been beheaded. This John had proclaimed Yeshua as Messiah, no less! This John, a man with a great following, had once insisted he was not even fit to untie the thongs of the teacher's sandals. And what had the teacher done for a prophet who had been beheaded at the request of a teenaged harlot? Nothing. The teacher, who Judas had seen command storms into silence, had not sent fire or earthquake or plague to destroy a man as evil as Herod, but instead had shared in grief with the others through prayer. Worse, later, the teacher had fled Galilee in fear of Herod.

Judas had brooded on this many nights near the flickering campfires in the countryside—until the miraculous feeding of the thousands on the far shore of the Sea of Galilee. In the joyous thunder of fervent hosannas that called the teacher to be king, Judas had found hope again, had swelled with pride to be one of the twelve closest to him.

To what end? Judas asked himself, his heart dominated by angry memories of the synagogue in Capernaum the day after the miracle of the feeding.

Yeshua that day was easily at the height of his popular support, and he had not taken the mantle, but had spurned the vast crowds, weaving no stories with his usual charismatic speech, but wearily telling them to drink his blood and eat his flesh.

Yes, the spy sent from the Pharisees had known well to touch upon this incident with Judas. In Capernaum back then, legions of followers had turned away, their disenchantment verging on disgust, for who could make sense of someone who claimed to be bread sent down from heaven?

Worse, in private conversation shortly after with the twelve, Yeshua had not only repeated the teachings, but had also turned to the group and accused one of being from the devil. It was as if Yeshua had spoken to the bitterness within Judas.

Could a man be blamed for turning love and hope into hatred at such a betrayal? Could a man be blamed for . . .

Anger drove Judas to walk faster and faster.

The chief priests awaited him.

30

While Judas's dark spirit drove him to the city and into the temple, mine eventually drove me out. I could contain my restlessness no longer.

I went to the theater, the horse races, the gymnasium, but all the entertainment failed to distract me.

Eventually my wanderings led me beneath the city.

Jerusalem's subterranean alleys are a world set apart from sunlight, laughter, and hope. They were built almost by accident as the city grew; it became easier to build on top of some of the ancient structures than to tear them down and haul the rubble away.

It is also a world of danger. Whispers bounce from unseen sources through the dim corridors. Movements are furtive. Shadows dance and are lost in deeper shadows. Thieves and assassins hunt each other and the weak.

Here, too, status means little. It is the refuge of the desperate, the unloved, and the poor who take comfort in shared misery and in escaping the shame that awaits them in sunlight.

Perhaps I wandered below the city following an unconscious wish to have the decision regarding my death taken from me.

If so, I failed that unacknowledged desire.

Before I had ventured a hundred steps into the darkness, two men stepped out from behind a pillar, daggers extended.

"Strip yourself," one snarled.

The other laughed. "You'll save us the work of pulling the clothes from your dead body."

So they wanted not only my possessions, but also my fear. I measured them.

They were pitiful. Small to begin with, hunger and alcohol had reduced them to grimy husks. They could not even hold their daggers steady. Had I turned and run, they would have collapsed within their first dozen steps of pursuit.

As they blustered more threats, I discovered that I was still capable of an emotion beyond the deadening sensation of guilt—anger.

Here was a place I could focus my frustration and hatred.

I roared and threw my right fist at the first man's head. Savage joy filled me at the pain of a popped knuckle. He fell immediately, sobbing.

The other had more spirit. He slashed at my right side, bouncing the edge of his dagger off my ribs, giving me more pain that burned a swath across my side and into the front of my consciousness.

Without thinking, I spun and lifted a knee, catching him in the midsection with such force that his feet left the ground. As he crashed onto his back, his head made a resounding thunk against the stone of the alley.

I stood poised to flail again, but neither moved.

I heaved for breath as I waited over them. The fight had been brief, but exertion in battle comes more from the mind's fear than the body's actions.

I felt my ribs. The dagger, rusted and dull, had not even cut through the cloth of my robe.

Between the sobs of the first man, I heard bubbling as he breathed through the blood that streamed from his nose. The other, I only half feared, was so inert as to be dead. Had I killed him, it would have mattered little. I would not have to face a court, and if I did, I would be applauded as a hero.

Yes. Wonderful me. Tall and well-nourished, I had defeated two broken men.

To further demonstrate the emptiness of my victory, a little girl pushed past my legs and fell upon the motionless man, crying and pleading for him to wake.

She was as grimy and pitiful as they. I became aware of their stench, a collective soured warmth on the damp coolness of the alley.

The man—I guessed her father—groaned. He was not dead, then.

Where my impulse came from, I do not know. My reputation is one of stern severity. While I do not pinch every shekel before I spend it, I do not spend foolishly and every bargain I drive is one that could not be driven harder or further. I was not known for charity. Yet here I was, moved for the second time since entering Jerusalem.

These two men were so utterly crushed, and the little girl's tears so wrenching, that I took my purse from beneath my robe.

I pulled the child up by an arm.

In the dim light, I saw only the shiny tracks of her tears etched through the dirt of her face.

She tried to pummel me with her fragile fists.

I caught both her wrists and squatted to look her as clearly in the eyes as the bad light permitted.

"This is for you," I said. I gave her the purse. Her feral eyes widened at the clink of shekels.

I did not wait for gratitude. I doubted it would come.

I also expected the men would take the money from her as soon as I departed. I only hoped the father, when he woke, would have the same fierce love for her that she had shown for him, and that he would spend some of the money on her.

I had learned my lesson in the alley and turned back, leaving the popping sound of bubbling blood.

As I reached the light, I discovered my guilt had eased. I felt an unfamiliar joy, and I began to wonder if I could shed my remorse like a snake's skin simply by unexpectedly granting gifts to those who had less than I.

But my joy did not last long.

Before I had stepped into the city proper, I remembered the blind beggar. I had given him more money than he expected in a month of tending his bowl, yet that largess had left me empty.

Why had I not felt this same joy with him?

It came to me. He was not a miserable young girl. But the young beggar, like my daughter, was.

When I realized this, my joy became ashes.

31

Too much of the afternoon remained. I went to the temple without sighting Yeshua and so decided to seek him among his friends. Against the flow of pilgrims making their way to Jerusalem, I walked up the Mount of Olives and down the ridge on the other side, past Bethpage, to Bethany. It had given me the chance to search for Yeshua among them. I had not seen him or his followers. From what I had heard, it seemed the best place to make inquiries would be at his friend's abode.

"Where is the house of Lazarus?" I asked a boy sitting on a pile of rocks at the side of the road.

The boy raised his smudged face to me, gave me a sly glance, then looked back down at his hand. He opened his fingers and a small lizard scooted to freedom.

"My hand is now empty," he said. "The lizard made room for a shekel."

"One shekel to give directions?"

The boy shrugged. "Many others have paid me to take them there."

So I was to be just one of many curiosity seekers. I should have expected it. Not many men are raised from the dead.

"Half a shekel," I told the boy.

He grinned. "Half a shekel. I'll take you there myself."

He'd spoken so quickly that I knew I'd paid too much, but other things occupied my mind.

He led me on a narrow path between the houses. Bethany was a small village. I could imagine it in the middle of the summer, the white walls of the single-level dwellings shimmering in the heat, weeds struggling for a foothold in the cracks between the rocks.

We rounded a corner and the boy pointed out a house with two goats tethered in front. "Half a shekel," he said.

"First," I answered. "Tell me if any share his house with him."

Another shrug. "Two old women. Mary and Martha."

I gave him his money and he dashed away, as if expecting me to call for it back.

I smiled when a woman with high cheekbones and a suspicious glance answered my call. The boy and I had differing opinions on what defined old. My guess was that she had not even reached her thirtieth year.

"What is it?" she asked without stepping out from the doorway. I smelled fresh bread baking inside.

"This is the house of Lazarus?"

"Yes," she answered. "And yes he was dead. Yes, he is now alive. No, it wasn't the work of the devil that brought him forth. And finally, even if he were here, he would be too busy to be poked and prodded."

A second woman appeared in the doorway. She was taller, slimmer, and younger. The same high cheekbones showed they were sisters, but this one did not have a face creased with suspicion.

"Martha," she told her older sister, "this poor man asked a simple question."

"Just as all the others have bothered us with simple questions to take us away from our work."

Before they could argue further, I slipped in another question. "I am actually looking for Yeshua. Do you know where he is?"

"No," Martha said firmly. "You have wasted your time."

Her sister placed a hand lightly on her forearm. Martha shook it off.

"See how he is dressed?" Martha said to her. "He's probably been sent by the Sadducees."

"No," I said.

The younger sister kept her eyes on my face as she spoke to Martha. "He has need of the teacher. Grant him some peace."

"The bread will burn. I have no time," Martha said as she stepped into the shadows of the house. She was out of my sight when she called her parting words from inside. "And Mary, you have your cleaning!"

"Forgive her," the woman in the doorway said. "She is worried these days for our teacher. It makes her short tempered."

"Worried for the teacher?"

"You have probably heard," Mary said. "After he healed our brother, the religious authorities called for his death. Yet he persists in going to the temple."

"Not today," I said. "I waited for him there."

"He has gone into the hills," she said. "He has taken a day of contemplation and quiet."

I was conscious of standing awkwardly in front of her. I was a man and a stranger; it would be improper to ask her to leave the house and join me in a walk. As she did not invite me in, I received a clear unspoken message. I was imposing upon her graciousness.

"My daughter is crippled," I blurted. It was a naked bid for her sympathy—appealing to her heart with news of a hurt child—but I was desperate. "He is my only hope."

"I tell you the truth," she replied. "I do not know where he is or when he will return."

Her eyes lingered on the mutilated left side of my face. I resisted the impulse to rub my scar.

"But he will return?" I persisted.

"He makes his plans known to no one. Spies are everywhere, and the religious authorities lie in wait to capture him away from the crowds."

I slumped. "How can he be the Messiah, then? How can he lead the nation if he lives in such fear?"

Mary understood that my questions were not meant as criticism. She answered softly.

"It is not fear. This leadership is what others want for him. He himself walks a different path."

I stared at her. "Who is he then?"

"We all ask that question," she said. "Even those closest to him."

"And you? What do you think?"

She smiled. "He is a man of love. One who not only heals people, but also forgives them of their sins and sets them free."

"No man has the power to forgive sins," I said.

"No man has the power to raise someone from the dead. Yet my brother walks and talks, even after four days in the tomb."

Four days' time was significant. Many of us Jews believed the soul stayed near the body for three days, waiting in hope that it might reenter the body. Not until the fourth day, we believed, did true death arrive with a drop of gall from the sword of the angel of death. This gall changed the body's face, forcing the soul to leave its resting place.

"If he can raise your brother," I said, "he can heal my daughter. I must see him."

"He does no one's bidding," Mary said. "Were I you, I would try to understand his teachings first."

In so many words, he had told me the same.

Martha called from inside the house. "Mary! Time grows short. We must prepare for the Passover."

Mary apologized for her sister with a quick grimace. "I wish I could help you more . . ."

"Please," I said, hiding my disappointment, "return to your sister. I will look for Yeshua in the temple later."

I turned back toward Jerusalem. For all the time and effort I had spent to visit Bethany, I had learned little. I should have expected Mary and Martha to confirm the raising of Lazarus; if it had been a carefully worked fraud, they would not reveal it to a passing stranger.

Even if I chose to believe in that unlikely miracle, it still brought me no closer to what I needed. Understand his teachings—there was nothing practical about that. This man seemed to be a whimsical, unpredictable mystic.

It was a shame, I thought, that neither money nor power seemed to tempt him. What could I do to bend his will to mine?

32

I fear for you," Pascal said. Seraphine had left us alone, disappearing after the meal to supervise servants. Candle flames wavered and made it difficult to read Pascal's face.

"Fear?" I smiled, as if his statement had not risen a snake's head of worry in my belly. *Has he or one of his servants found my letters to Jaala?*

He sighed. "Surely by now you understand that a fly does not land in this city without my knowledge. Take your hand, for example. The knuckles, bruised and scraped. The way you wince with every movement. Even had I not heard about your encounter with the thieves, I would have noticed something during our meal tonight."

"Pascal, I will find it unforgivable if you had me followed during the day." I had told no one of the happenings in the ally beneath the city. If he knew it was because he had made efforts to track my movements.

Pascal sighed again. "Must I remind you of your appearance? How long do you think it took for word to spread through the underbelly of this city that an expensively dressed unarmed man with a distinctive scar attacked two with knives and defeated them?"

My smile was grim, unamused. "You have friends among thieves."

"Don't be a fool. Of course I do." He grinned, trying to relieve the tension between us. "Most of them live here in the upper city."

I was not in the mood. Neither was he; his grin faded.

"Admit it," Pascal said. "During any of your other visits, your mind found nothing of interest but the price of glass, silk, and other luxuries. You worked ceaselessly, securing shipments at prices far below market rates. Yet this past week, the only mention you've made of business is a cryptic offer to sell what you own, and even then, you've ignored any opportunity to discuss that offer with me further."

"Other matters seemed more important. I will make a list of the assets tomorrow and present it to you before the Passover begins."

"I'm not sure that will be necessary—which is why I fear for you."

"I don't understand," I said.

He rubbed his face pensively before looking at me again. "You went to Bethany today. You made inquiries at the house of Lazarus. Do you deny this?"

I half stood, immediately angry.

He put up a tired hand. "Simeon, I did not have you followed. The Sanhedrin have spies everywhere around this man. As always, their reports reached me through friends of mine."

I remained half standing.

"Sit. Please," Pascal urged. "Understand that I am willing to see things from your point of view. I have never had the joy of a child, let alone a son to carry my name. I can only imagine how deeply it would hurt to lose him had God given me such a gift . . ."

For all my anger and for all my faults, even I could recognize that Pascal had acknowledged his own deepest pain, sorrow, and shame, the lack of an heir. Seraphine was his fourth wife; he was long past being able to blame a barren womb instead of his own infertile seed.

I sat, as weary as he was.

"A good charlatan can deceive the best, and I pray that in your grief you have not fallen into this Yeshua's power," Pascal said. I had never seen his face so softened with the gentleness I saw in the candlelight. The quietness of his voice matched the compassion of his gaze. "I think of you as a brother, and it would break my heart to see that the rumors of a man raised from the dead have led you to false hope."

"You need not worry about me."

Pascal shook his head and tightened his lips in sadness. "Simeon, listen to me. He cannot bring your son back. Nor can he heal your daughter."

"I'm not sure I wish to continue this discussion."

"We must," he said. His face had lost none of its concern for me. "The Sanhedrin believe you want to join Yeshua's movement, and that leaves me no choice. I cannot consider any dealings with you, at least not now. In a year perhaps, when this false messiah has been forgotten. But not now. I hope you understand."

Before I could reply, Pascal continued. "What makes this conversation so difficult is that your interest in the false messiah has been in vain."

I waited.

"One of his followers visited the temple today," Pascal

said. He carefully watched my face. "Obviously a shrewd man, he sees the end. I assume he knows that if he helps the religious authorities, they can't prosecute him later."

Pascal's narration was not one of triumph, but resignation. "Think of it. The chief priests are deep in discussions that must not be recorded by any scribes. Their priority issue, of course, is this prophet from Galilee, who threatens each of their areas of temple jurisdiction. He must be stopped. But he is too popular. If he is taken publicly, the people will riot. Pilate will send in his troops. But how can he be taken in secret when he comes and goes so unpredictably? Then this man Judas approaches and offers them the prophet."

Pascal shook his head in mild disgust. "Our holy representatives did not merely accept the gift but still fought for a bargain. To get this Yeshua would be worth half the temple treasury. Yet they bartered until Judas agreed to betray his master for the legal price of a slave."

I felt the muscles in my chest squeeze.

"Betray?" I echoed.

"The prophet will die. And the price of his life was only thirty pieces of silver."

33

As I stared sightlessly in the darkness, lost in my miserable world, much higher stakes politics took place not far from my guest chamber.

After all, no place was far from another here in the wealthy upper quarters of Jerusalem. Pascal's mansion lay roughly halfway between the palace of Caiaphas the high priest and Herod's Palace, where the Roman governor of Judea sequestered himself when he stayed in the city.

And, as best as I can guess from what I later learned from a bow-legged Greek servant, at some time during my thoughts, Caiaphas himself must have passed nearby—in secrecy, in darkness, without guards—on his way to see a man named Pontius Pilate. . . .

Caiaphas waited with concealed impatience in the warm room of the bathhouse in Herod's Palace. He knew exactly why Pontius Pilate had chosen the location for this meeting— the heated, moist air made waiting uncomfortable for anyone dressed in full clothing. Furthermore, Pilate wanted it clear every moment that Rome ruled, and his possession of the palace built by Herod the Great said it much more eloquently and pervasively than words. Finally, Pontius Pilate enjoyed lording his physical prowess over others.

The floor and walls of the warm room were tiled with exquisite mosaics, and an elegant low table stood against the far wall. Other than that, the room was empty. Heavy grunts and groans from the hot room and the roar of the furnace below that heated water to steam was all that distracted Caiaphas from his thoughts.

Caiaphas knew why the location was chosen, but not why the meeting had been called, nor the hour for it. His spies, who informed him of every public move made by Pilate, as well as most of his private ones, had told Caiaphas nothing unusual. What could be so important that Pilate did not wait until morning?

Fifteen minutes passed. Caiaphas refused to mop his brow, even as his clothing grew heavy from moisture. To torment him more, his palate began to click with dryness, and the insides of his thighs began to itch with the beginning of a rash.

Still, he had enough discipline to hold himself tall and rigid as the grunts and groans continued just out of sight. The barbarians spent too much time in the hedonistic pleasure of muscle massage and skin scraping.

The first indication that Pilate was ready came when his servant, a large bow-legged Greek, stepped out of the hot room and scurried past Caiaphas. Pontius Pilate arrived moments later with a towel wrapped loosely around his lower belly and legs. He held the towel with his left hand, making no effort to hide the stubs of his first two fingers, each long ago sheered at the first knuckle and healed like blunt sausages.

"So," Pilate said. He looked Caiaphas up and down, making it obvious that his soldier's judgment found Caiaphas utterly weak.

Pontius Pilate was wide and thick, almost totally dark with chest and stomach hair beaded with water droplets. Long, narrow scars—sword and spear—covered his upper arms and shoulders. His gleaming red face held full lips beneath a nose crooked from a poorly healed break. The hair that crowned his head formed a bowl in classical Roman cut.

Caiaphas hated Pilate for his smug reliance on the bearlike power of a middle-aged body not yet soft from age. Caiaphas hated as well the intimacy of standing in the presence of a nearly naked man. Most of all, Caiaphas hated the feeling of inferiority and weakness that Pilate inspired.

"So, High Priest," Pilate said, "Passover is upon us. Once again, the Jews celebrate a miracle that let them cast off the shackles of subjection to a world power."

Caiaphas felt the first wave of dizziness overcome him. Standing in the heat had taken its toll.

"Yet here you are," Pontius continued, "in shackles again. Roman shackles."

The servant returned carrying a heated pot of oil in a thick towel.

Pontius Pilate dropped his own towel, and smirked at Caiaphas's stony, straight-ahead look. He walked to the table, settled on his belly, and allowed the servant to begin oiling the skin of his back.

"Isn't it wonderful to be enemies?" Pilate said. "We can trust that we distrust. We can love our hatreds. Each side knows where the other stands because each side watches the other as surely as if they were lovers."

In the dizzying heat, Caiaphas had to widen his stance to keep his balance.

"And this is what I know," Pilate said. "A few years ago, when a delegation of Jews came to Caesarea to protest the military insignias in Antonia above the temple, you were not among them. They were prepared to die before leaving, yet you, their religious leader, conveniently remained in Jerusalem."

Pilate hummed with pleasure for a few moments as the servant continued to knead oil onto his broad muscles.

"I know, too, that you and I agreed to have the Romans build an aqueduct into Jerusalem with temple funds," Pilate said, "and that once it was built, you then made it appear to the populace that we had robbed the temple."

Pilate closed his eyes. "And since then, I know that you sent word to Tiberius, going over my head, to protest the gold shields that honored him, not within the temple where I could understand any claims of sacrilege, but here in the hall of this palace."

Pilate opened his eyes again. "As I see it, you do not fight openly as an honorable soldier, but hidden, as a snake in the reeds."

"I doubt you requested my presence at this hour to go over old history that reflects more your poor judgment than any failings of my own actions." Caiaphas allowed a smirk to rest on his own face. There had been rumors of a letter from Tiberius, the unpredictable dictator from Rome. "I suspect, if anything, you are an honorable soldier about to lose your position as governor if news of any more Judean disturbances reaches your beloved Tiberius. And because of that, you need my help to keep the peace."

By Pilate's sudden, rigid silence, Caiaphas realized his jibe had hit the mark.

Pilate recovered, but too late. "Isn't hatred refreshing? Who would have thought a dried-up old Jew could harbor the passion that you do. Let us keep this hatred out in the open, where it fools no one."

"Why did you call me here?" Caiaphas asked. "Surely not to establish that I need you. Or you me. We have known that for years. It seems to work rather well, as long as we each stay out of the other's way."

"Then we shall speak plainly," Pilate said. "I have brought in extra garrisons of soldiers for the Passover. See that I need not bring them into use."

"What could you possibly imagine as trouble?"

"Anything that involves Jews," Pilate snapped. "Let me repeat myself. I want no trouble. Do you understand?"

Caiaphas understood. The letter from Tiberius was more than rumor. Pilate could afford no more trouble, or he would be recalled in shame to Rome. And as more than a rumor, it gave Caiaphas the leverage he needed in future dealings with Pilate.

The smile that played at the corners of Caiaphas's mouth was not directed at Pilate, but against another.

Caiaphas had his betrayer. Now he had the power to direct Pilate's judgment.

Thus armed, a man of hate could dream of triumph against the man of love.

THURSDAY

34

My dearest love,

The stylus is now in my hand. However, just moments ago, I was not thinking of words to send you, but holding yesterday's letter near a candle flame. By burning it, I would have kept you from hearing how far I have fallen in the seemingly hopeless pursuit of reclaiming our lives.

But I promised you my honesty. That commitment kept me from thrusting the scroll into the flame. So, by the time a servant reads you this letter, you will know that in the dark of night, I actually wondered if the Messiah had arrived among us. I actually hoped he might heal Vashti.

I have lost that hope. He is only an ordinary man, betrayed in squalid circumstance, about to die an insignificant death.

It probably matters little to our circumstances. If I am promising honesty, I must admit to you—and to me—that I am not sure that I could have found my way back to you, even had he restored Vashti's legs.

I could probably rightly say that your unspoken blame has been a wall between us since the fire. It is a wall I believe now I could have climbed if not for the burden I dared not share.

I have never been unfaithful to you. But I imagine it is no different for a husband who has strayed. His wife may never know of the infidelity, but for the man, it is a secret of shame that festers and drives him away in hundreds of small ways.

As too, my burden. How could I allow you to love me when I hated myself? So I allowed the little love that remained between us to be slowly destroyed.

I cannot hope in the Messiah.

Because I foolishly pursued that hope, I cannot expect to sell my estates to Pascal as I had planned.

What do I have left?

Nothing.

The daughter who once sang loving lullabies to me, the daughter who once whispered silly things in my ear—she now screams with agony and will not even meet my eyes when I attempt to comfort her.

The son who once climbed my back and shouted with glee, the son who once followed me in the shops, imitating my every move—he is now cold and still and alone in a tomb.

And you? All I have are my memories. Once sweet, and now more bitter because of the sweetness I shall never taste again.

I have no peace.

Today I begin the final steps to reclaim peace. Not in pursuit of a charlatan messiah. But by my own efforts.

You are my love. I have asked before and I ask again: Pray for me. Against the chance that there is no God, I must hold the chance that there is. It cannot hurt for you to place your heart before him on my behalf. If there is no one to listen, neither of us has lost anything. Because we cannot lose any more than what we already have lost.

And for what we have lost, I will pay the price to set us both free.

35

Shortly after the dawn's trumpets called the city to prayer, I began to walk the streets, paying little attention to where my feet took me. Because I had long since chosen to deny myself wine as escape, and because I could not sleep and thus find refuge from myself, it seemed my only relief came in movement.

It was poor relief.

I took no pleasure in the beauty of the soft blue sky above, scrubbed clear by the rain that had passed through the mountains. Lungfuls of the morning's cool air did not invigorate my blood.

As for my other senses, food was tasteless paste. The thought of fleshly pleasures left me cold; no woman's embrace but my wife's mattered, and even if I returned to her, she would never offer me open arms.

Despair congealed around my heart.

So I walked.

I descended from my cousin's mansion in the upper quarters. I crossed over the aqueduct that marked the lower boundary of the wealthy and restlessly wandered into the crowded filth of the lower city, barely aware of the pain of those hunched in doorways or limping through tiny alleys with staggering loads on their backs.

My feet kept me in motion. I reached the main street of the lower quarter. Had I turned left, I would have passed the temple, then the Roman fortress on its northwest corner. Farther on stood the blacksmith shops, the wool shops, the clothes market near the underground quarries at the north end of the city.

I did not make a conscious decision to turn right, but I moved slowly in the direction of the Siloam Pool. Fifteen or twenty minutes later, I reached the end of a street where the outer city wall abruptly blocked my progress. Built for defense, it was easily higher than the flat-roofed houses it contained in this corner of Jerusalem, wide enough that a horse could pull a cart along its top edge.

I stared at the heavy stones for several minutes.

With a grim smile, I realized I had indeed found my destination. A set of narrow, rough steps jutted out from the wall, leading to the top. I climbed, and since the outer edge had no support rails, I leaned for balance against the wall to guard against a painful fall. That, considering my intentions, struck me as ironic.

From the top of the wall, I surveyed the breathtaking drop down the sheer cliff of the Kidron Valley. A half mile to my left was the temple, towering over the poverty within its shadows. Ahead and across the valley stood the Mount of Olives, dark against the rising sun behind it.

But it was the drop that held my attention.

Idly, I kicked a small rock into the vast emptiness. It fell with the swiftness I expected, but as it gained distance, it seemed to float until finally, a dozen heartbeats later, it clattered off the boulders below.

That could be me, I thought. In that short a time, I could have total escape from my miserable life. With a slight flex of my legs and the small price of the brief flash of a smashed skull, I could leave behind all that weighed my soul.

How badly did I want to live? Less than a day before, my fury against the thieves had shown me the spark was bright.

Yet . . .

I saw again the oil spilled across my daughter's legs, and the snakelike flame licking the path of the oil. I saw again my son's body, the fragment of cloth clutched in his small hand.

I swayed on the edge of the wall with my arms lifted against the breeze.

Yes, I thought. I could do it. I could step out into the emptiness and welcome my death as the air tore at my robe and the boulders rushed toward me.

I might find peace. Not yet, though.

First, I needed to ensure that Jaala and Vashti would not become paupers in the wake of my departure. If Pascal would not purchase my estates while I was alive, he would find it easily possible after my death.

It is fanciful to think that my solitary figure on the wall would have drawn the attention of thirteen men in their place of refuge.

As a bird flies, however, I was closer to them than to the temple. And I was as unaware of them as they were of me—until events of the future compelled me to learn what I could. . . .

They rested in a garden at the base of the Mount of Olives.

The walls of the garden contained a hundred gnarled, ancient olive trees—ten rows of ten in a rough square spaced several paces apart, each with a gray, weathered trunk double the thickness of a man's body and hardly taller than double a man's reach. From the massive trunks, webs of low wide-spreading branches reached out, shading the garden with the delicate patterns of their tendrils of new shoots and curls of new green leaves.

Gethsemane, nearby residents called it, the garden of the oil press. It was a garden in the traditional sense as well, for while its owner made profit from the olive oil he sold for cooking and lamp fuel, he saw no reason to leave the open ground surrounding the trees barren, and had planted small fruit trees and flowering shrubs. Later in the heat of the year, with everything in bloom, it would be a medicine of peace to sit in the honeysuckled sweetness of an early morning.

As it was still early, however, the peace of the garden came not from blossoms, but from the timeless dignity of the scarred solidness of the olive trees, the new grass, the still air, and the distant burbling of the Kidron.

Here, Yeshua rested with his disciples. Nearby, tied by a halter to a low-hanging branch of an olive tree, the white lamb that Judas had purchased the day before tugged at the grass, unmindful of the men nearby.

All reclined against the tree trunks—but one.

Judas. He had been walking the garden ever since the disciples had arrived following their early meal of leavened bread.

He was thirty pieces of silver richer, but there remained the problem of earning that silver. He had to arrange a time and location where the authorities could arrest Yeshua.

This was no easy matter. Worried about riots, the chief priests had instructed Judas it must be a private place.

This garden and this morning, of course, would have been perfect. But if Judas left now, there was no certainty that Yeshua and the others would still be in the garden when the religious authorities arrived.

No, Judas needed to know a time and place ahead of time. Especially since that would allow Judas to be among the disciples when the authorities appeared, leaving him unsuspected as the betrayer.

But, Judas asked himself again and again, *how can I know where Yeshua will be?*

When the solution struck Judas, it was so obvious that he smiled. He hid his urgency as he walked toward Yeshua, who leaned comfortably against a tree, smiling, eyes closed, face tilted to the sun.

As Judas's shadow fell upon Yeshua, the teacher opened his eyes.

"We must begin to prepare for the Passover supper," Judas said. "As you know, room is scarce in the city. Let me tend to our arrangements."

Nothing about Yeshua's expression changed, but slowly, tears filled his eyes as he looked wordlessly at Judas. Judas felt an unspoken reproach. *Had the impossible happened? Had someone seen him enter the palace of the high priest? Had someone drawn the easy conclusion and informed Yeshua? Or was his own conscience so plain upon his face?*

A black shivering void swept through Judas. A void brought on by his urgency to betray and by the fear of the magnitude of that betrayal. A void brought on by his possible failure. And by his possible success. Judas tried to cover his cold dizziness by pushing the conversation.

"I am the keeper of the common purse," Judas said. He had planned his arguments. He hoped his voice didn't tremble. "And I know how important this Passover supper is to—"

"No." Yeshua shook his head at Judas. His voice was quiet. The other disciples would not overhear. "Yesterday, you went into the city and purchased the lamb. You have already done enough."

You have already done enough.

Should he look for a double meaning in the teacher's words?

Yeshua closed his eyes again and tilted his head back to the tree.

Later Judas would convince himself that if only Yeshua had not dismissed him, he would have returned the silver to Caiaphas that morning. Instead he stepped away, his face burning with shame and anger, his alienation heightening his sense of determination.

If the other disciples noticed the quiet conversation, none showed interest. Judas wandered deep into the garden, thinking only thoughts of self-pity.

The others continued to rest.

And the lamb, unaware of the few hours left to its short, innocent life, remained content in the new grass.

The echo of silver trumpets rang through Jerusalem, signaling to the pilgrims that the eating of leavened bread must cease. This early division of the festive day, however, was strictly a rabbinical hedge of safety. Not for another two hours would the official abstention begin.

The same echo of trumpets reached Gethsemane. Yeshua rose from his comfortable meditative position. He called for Peter and John.

His voice, after the long silence, naturally drew the attention of the rest of the disciples. Judas moved closer, too, but still found himself on the outside fringe.

"Teacher?" Peter asked.

"Go and make preparations for us to eat the Passover," Yeshua said. His voice held not command, but near resignation.

"Where do you want us to prepare for it?" John asked.

Judas leaned forward, straining to hear the answer. His heart thumped and he swallowed hard, as if this were the actual moment of betrayal. Now, he would get the answer he needed. And later, he would find an excuse to slip away and deliver the information to the authorities.

Yeshua will be defeated.

"Go into the city and a man carrying a jar of water will meet you," Yeshua said. He looked past Peter and John briefly, catching Judas's intense interest. "Follow him. When he goes into a house, tell the owner of the house, 'The teacher says: Where is my guest room in which I can eat the Passover meal with my followers?' The owner will show you a large room upstairs that is furnished and ready. Prepare the food for us there."

Judas saw plainly that Peter and John exchanged quick frowns of mutual puzzlement. Anger stabbed him with a dagger of savage heat. They were so close—these two Galileans—and shared an intimacy they never would with him, the outsider Judean.

The real heat of Judas's bitterness, however, came from something far more significant.

Neither Peter nor John—nor the other disciples—understood why Yeshua's instructions were so vague.

Judas, however, knew.

Carrying water was woman's work, out of the ordinary for a man, an extraordinarily simple method to make a man recognizable. As simple as the method of choosing the trumpet call as the time for the man with the water to go forth and be found.

Yes, Judas knew.

Yeshua must have already made arrangements for a room for the Passover supper; Yeshua must have already planned this simple method of connecting as a way to keep the location unnamed ahead of time.

Judas knew. Yeshua had not only foreseen Judas's intentions, but had also taken steps to thwart him.

And Judas knew even more.

Yeshua remained in control.

Judas blinded his heart to his deepening shame by covering it with a blanket of hatred.

36

I climbed off the wall, knowing I still had business to attend to. The rest of the morning held less pain; I had, for the moment, a purpose. I searched out a lawyer and dictated to him the contents of an agreement I intended to deliver to Pascal.

The lawyer's fees were double what I would have paid had my thoughts not been lured by the prospect of death from the temple wall. The lawyer had protested it was too close to Passover to finish the document on time—I was so distracted I did not bother to fight such an obvious ploy for extra fees.

I left the lawyer with a scroll in the sleeve of my robe and returned to the mansion of my cousin, where I hid the scroll with the letters for my wife. Thus suspended from the sharper edges of torment, I managed to wait on a couch in a cool inner chamber until Pascal called for me. Together we made our way to the temple for the sacrifice of our Passover lamb.

There was no enmity between us. I understood the practical reasons why he could not purchase my holdings, and indeed found it a comfort that he insisted that we remain together in the temple despite the raised eyebrows my presence drew when his Sadducee friends greeted us.

Among the crowd in the temple, I would have recognized the disciple named Peter had I seen him; his rigid rejection of my offer for money had left a vivid memory. The crowd around us was too thick, so I did not see him or the other disciple named John.

They were close by, however. Waiting, as we were, for the gates to the altar to open. . . .

In front of the massive Nicanor Gates inside the temple courts, Peter held the lamb that Judas had purchased. He and John were hemmed in by a packed crowd of noisy pilgrims, all of whom represented groups waiting to celebrate the Passover feast that evening.

On the other side of the tall, heavy doors, the Priest's Court was filling with hundreds of white-robed priests and Levites as they prepared for the afternoon ceremonies; this was the one day each year that every temple priest was called to duty at the sacrificial altars.

While the trussed lamb in Peter's arms remained silent, the bleating of other lambs rose above the babble of the crowd. The musky smell of the lambs mixed with the pungent aroma of fresh dung and the general odor of hundreds of people sweating in the afternoon heat. Of this dense crowd, it seemed to Peter that only he and John were silent. Peter could only guess that John felt the same terrible loneliness, for neither had the heart to discuss with the other his sense of foreboding.

Without realizing it, Peter soothed the animal in his arms with slow strokes along its neck and back, as if trying to allay his own fears.

As Yeshua had predicted, there had been a manservant carrying a water jar. And as Yeshua had predicted, the servant's master—the father of young Mark, a follower of Yeshua—had shown them an upper chamber ready for the Passover.

Earlier, Yeshua had correctly foretold where they would find a young donkey. And that they would be able to take it simply by asking.

And more than once, Yeshua had predicted his own crucifixion. That the other predictions had been fulfilled seemed to Peter ominous evidence of Yeshua's accurate sense of the future. And yesterday Yeshua had predicted his own crucifixion.

Crucifixion. The end of their teacher. The end of their dreams.

Peter even held a sense of danger for himself and John. After all, once the gate opened and they lined up before the priests on the other side, it seemed easily possible that either or both might be recognized as followers of Yeshua. These were the religious authorities who had posted notice that Yeshua must be reported if seen in public. For that reason, Peter and John, in the manner of their Galilean countrymen, had each hidden short swords beneath their upper garments.

Peter became conscious that, in his nervousness, he had been stroking the lamb. For the first time in his adult life, he became aware of an animal as a fellow creature; the rough fisherman's life in Galilee did not allow for the luxury of considering animals as more than beasts of burden, sacrifices, or food. Peter ran his thick fingers through the lamb's delicate wool, watching how its thickness parted and fell back, marveling at the softness of its hair. He felt the animal's warmth against his arms and stomach, felt the quick thudding of the lamb's heart against his ribs, noticed the liquid depths of its wide eyes. The lamb was tiny, helpless. To Peter's surprise, a tenderness surged within him. The big, strong, stubborn fisherman swelled with sympathy for the lamb and its fate.

And ahead, priests finally began to open the gates.

The anticipation was twofold. Passover was different from the regular sacrifices because ordinary people participated in the ritual killing; it was also one of the few yearly occasions when Israelite worshipers were allowed to enter the priests' inner temple domain.

The size of the altar was enough to silence any pilgrim entering for the first time. The altar had been built on the same site on Mount Moriah where centuries earlier Abraham had bound his son Isaac for slaughter. The altar was a perfect square of stones and earth, twice the height of a house, with an ascent ramp leading to the top where three fires burned. The largest—for burning sacrifices—was a pile of glowing, crackling wood taller than the priests tending it with long metal tongs.

Pascal and I shuffled with the crowd through the gates into the inner temple. As did, somewhere behind us among the massed crowd, Peter and John.

The court filled and priests closed the gates again. Later, a second wave of pilgrims would enter. Then a third. Peter and John had hurried to be in the first group as they were anxious to leave quickly to meet Yeshua and the others in the upper room promised them.

Inside, priests lined the steps of the altar, from top to bottom in a long double row that spilled beyond the steps to the center of the court.

Each priest had gone through a lengthy purification process

of cleansing and ritual. Each was ready for his sacred duty. The spilling of blood.

A threefold blast from the silver trumpets of the priests echoed against the hewn marble and stones. There was a pause, like a heartbeat stopped. And then, like a heartbeat pulsing back to life, hundreds of Levites began the ancient chant of the Hallel.

"Praise the Lord!" they called. The deep symphony of male voices rolled across the inner court.

"Praise the Lord!" the pilgrims chanted in return.

The Levites continued the verses of the psalms. The pilgrims only repeated the first line of each psalm. Every other line they responded to by singing hallelujah.

The repetitive hallelujahs and the mesmerizing chant of the hundreds of Levites raised us to an emotional level of yearning joy, an awesome inner movement of souls stirred to reach for God.

As the chant rose and fell, the first pilgrims at the base of the altar began to sacrifice the animals they had brought with them. The priest at the front of each line caught the blood of the dying animal in a golden bowl, and passed the bowl to the priest behind him, getting in return an empty bowl. The priest behind passed the blood-filled bowl back. Each new bowl went up the long line of priests, until the final priest threw the blood in a spray at the base of the great fire of the altar and passed that bowl back down again.

No Gentile would ever witness this; the penalty was death for a non-Jew who dared defile the inner temple with his presence. Only Jews could see the slaughter of thousands of lambs and the river of their innocent blood.

I could not fool myself, of course, into placing any hope in this ritual. I was only here because I had to maintain an untroubled pose until I had departed from Pascal's household. As for the fierce disciple with red hair . . .

The chanting flowed over Peter and moved him in a way he'd never been moved. Because of his unexpected tenderness toward the lamb in his arms, this was the first Passover in which he truly began to understand in his heart what he had been taught in the synagogues since childhood. With his unexpected sorrow for the lamb's destiny and the reason for its death, an awareness of God's love began to fill the crevices of Peter's soul.

It was a mystical moment. Peter looked up to the cloudless sky, half expecting to see in the sun the blinding brightness of God's face.

In his arms, the lamb began to twist and struggle in panic as it smelled the fear and blood of the dying animals ahead. With his new understanding of the significance of sacrifice, it pained Peter to hold the lamb prisoner as he and John moved up in the line of pilgrims.

"This is the day the Lord has made," the Levites chanted in the strange thunderous roar of men caught up in the vicarious taste of death. "Let us rejoice and be glad in it."

And the people around Peter and John shouted in return. *Hallelujah*.

At the priest's feet, Peter knelt with John. Peter pressed the struggling lamb's fragile body against the floor of the court. The priest's flowing white robe was soaked with blood.

O Lord, save us. O Lord, grant us success.

And the people shouted in return. *Hallelujah*.

With one hand against the lamb's head, and with a knife in his other hand, John slashed through the quivering tendons of the lamb's neck to slit its throat. As the lamb thrashed, blood jetted in spurts against his sleeve and Peter's.

Blessed is he who comes in the name of the Lord.

And the people shouted in return. *Hallelujah.*

The awareness of the warmth of the blood against Peter's arm mingled with the wonderful awareness of his soul, which now seemed to flutter—like the torn muscles of the lamb's neck—between incredible joy and incredible sadness. As the lamb's blood flowed into the golden bowl, and as the lamb's life drained away, Peter's voice rose in *hallelujahs* with the tumult around him.

Peter wept in the beauty of the moment.

Hosanna in the highest. Hosanna in the highest.

And the people shouted in return. *Hallelujah.*

Peter averted his face from John as they stood. The tears ran into his beard, and with his hands occupied by the burden of the dead lamb, he could not wipe them away.

John made no comment.

All that remained was to lay the sacrificed lamb on staves, where other priests would expertly skin it, removing the innards for burning at the altar, and taking care that the bones of the lamb not be broken.

Later, as Peter and John walked through the city with the lamb's carcass on a wood frame between them, the sight of hundreds of special ovens set in public places for the pilgrims' use brought back the memory of the sacrifice. And something else surged in Peter's memory.

Blessed is he who comes in the name of the Lord.

Hallelujah.

Hosanna in the highest. Hosanna in the highest.
Hallelujah.

Those same triumphant cries—the cries heard over the dying lamb—had also rung through the valley on Sunday as thousands had cheered Yeshua's approach to Jerusalem.

THURSDAY EVENING

37

I would argue that where faith or meaning diminishes, ritual fills the void. The Passover supper commemorated my people's last meal in Egypt before the Exodus led by Moses; I imagine to the generation that first celebrated it, gratitude mattered far more than layers of ceremony. To them, a roasted lamb and unleavened bread were sufficient reminders of their newfound freedom and the angel of death that passed over their firstborn for the sake of lamb's blood smeared on their doorframes.

I, on the other hand, found myself prisoner to centuries of adornment as I reclined at the Passover supper with Pascal and Seraphine. I squirmed with boredom as prescribed prayer and hymns followed the order that had been regulated by dusty old men with dusty old scrolls. Where among these rites was the spirit of a mighty God who had inflicted plagues, parted the sea, and rained desert manna upon a people unworthy of his considerations?

I did not mention these thoughts to Pascal as he raised the first cup of wine for a traditional prayer. It was easier to suffer in silence than deal with the questions my thoughts would have provoked. After all, from his point of view, it would have been too surprising to discover that after showing myself as a ruthless merchant of glass and silk, I was suddenly wasting time in philosophical discourse.

And, because I did not want to draw the least amount of attention to myself, I drank from my goblet. It was the first wine I had tasted in months. When I wiped a few drops from the corner of my mouth with the back of my wrist, it looked like blood gleaming in the candlelight.

I would think of that sight later when I heard the account of another Passover supper that began in a hidden room in Jerusalem as our own Passover meal drew to an end. . . .

As the disciples followed Yeshua into the upper chamber, they saw the table set according to Passover custom.

Jewish law specifically dictated that pilgrims not sit at the meal but recline on their left elbow and side, leaving the right hand free to eat. Such positioning of the guests made it impossible for a servant to reach over them to serve. Because of this, the upper two-thirds of the elongated oval table was surrounded by a horseshoe of cushions, and the extended lower third held the Passover dishes—unleavened bread, bitter herbs, radish, and vinegar in a bowl—within reach.

Yeshua, lost in thought, moved to the cushion customarily held for the head of the table. On the left side, it was the second cushion from the end, deemed the middle. John took the end cushion, immediately to the right of Yeshua, below the master's feet.

The others moved to various other cushions as Peter, who had supervised the roasting of the lamb, set the meat beside the other dishes. This gave Judas a chance to squeeze past Peter and unhurriedly take the cushion above Yeshua, to the master's left. The place of honor.

Peter waited for Yeshua to command Judas to move.

Instead, Yeshua took the first of the four cups of wine that were to fulfill the Passover and began the formal ceremonial benedictions. Peter had no choice but to finally recline on the empty cushion directly across from John. The place of least honor.

Divine serenity filled Yeshua. All things were under his power as given by the Father; he had come from God and would return to God. With majestic dignity, he continued the prayer.

"Take this cup and share it among yourselves," he said, passing the cup. "I will not drink again from the fruit of the vine until God's kingdom comes."

The disciples exchanged puzzled glances, but Yeshua passed the first cup, and the disciples dipped herbs in the vinegar.

Yeshua took one of the three flat cakes of unleavened bread and broke it, putting some aside, as custom dictated, for after supper. It was also custom at this moment for the youngest to ask the reason for Passover. Yeshua answered, telling the story of Moses and the first Passover. When he finished, the men joined their voices to sing hallels from the ancient psalms.

Yeshua reached for the second ceremonial cup of wine and began the traditional prayers. The meal resumed after the second cup of wine had been passed, and Yeshua looked around the table as the others ate.

"One of you will turn against me," he said, "one of you who eats with me now."

Some of the disciples froze, hands halfway to their mouths. Others set the unleavened bread down and stared at Yeshua.

It took a half minute before anyone recovered enough to break the silence.

"Surely not I?" two asked, their words overlapping.

"It is one of the twelve—one who dips his bread into the bowl with me." Trouble filled the master's face. He was unable to speak with much strength as emotion choked him. "The Son of Man will die, just as the Scriptures say. But how terrible it will be for the person who hands the Son of Man over to be killed. It would be better for him if he had never been born."

The table filled with the babble of each disciple twisting and turning and speaking at once.

In this noise, Judas leaned over and spoke softly to Yeshua across the short space that separated them. "Surely not I," he said, deliberately echoing the words of the others to avoid their attention. *How could Yeshua have known?*

The light in Yeshua's eyes fragmented to shards of pain. Although he stared at Judas, it was as if he saw beyond to a night of utmost loneliness, a night with the monstrous depths of hell at his feet, with the fires of torment licking at the edges of the soul.

Yeshua did not answer Judas immediately. His silence, perhaps, was a final appeal to Judas to turn back from the fires of a soul damned to eternal separation from God.

Judas waited, barely breathing, not using the long silence to ponder Yeshua's warning of woe to the betrayer, but selfishly hoping for confirmation that Yeshua did not suspect him.

"Yes, it is you," Yeshua said softly.

Judas recoiled and waited for Yeshua to tell the others.

Yeshua simply bowed his head and retreated into himself.

Judas told himself that he imagined the slight tremble of Yeshua's chest, just as he convinced himself that Yeshua had misunderstood the question above the noise at the rest of the table.

For Judas, it would be unbearable to see that Yeshua wept silently and without tears. Just as it would be unbearable to think that Yeshua actually knew his plans.

38

At the meal's end, the oily smell of roasted lamb clung to our clothing; custom demanded that we burn all parts left over, and with only three of us, much of the lamb had gone uneaten, to sizzle and spit smoky grease as the fire devoured it.

"I have made arrangements with my friend Caiaphas," Pascal said abruptly. "Shortly, one of his servants will arrive to escort you back to his palace."

Seraphine's puzzled look reflected my own response.

"For what purpose?" I asked.

"Have you forgotten our conversation yesterday evening? The prophet has been betrayed. His arrest will happen tonight. I want you among the priests and soldiers."

"I am tired," I said. "It is not something I wish to do."

"It is a chance to redeem yourself," he persisted.

I laughed. Neither understood.

"You must be seen with the priests," he continued. "My Sadducee friends must know you are for them, not him. Once they are satisfied of your allegiance, you and I can begin discussing the matter you brought before me at the beginning of the week."

I shook my head no. I'd already made my decision on how to dispose of my estate. "I am tired."

"Tired? Or afraid to discover that your man of miracles is not a man of miracles? Tonight you will know one way or another. Your own eyes will give witness."

There was a reason Pascal was among the wealthiest in Jerusalem. He knew exactly how to manipulate a man's weakness.

And he had found mine.

When the servant arrived within the hour, I made the short journey to the palace of the high priest.

We waited for the arrival of the one named Judas. He was about to be sent by Yeshua . . .

When the noise of conversation died, Yeshua referred again to a betrayer.

"I am not talking about all of you," he said, trouble and pain thickening his words. "I know those I have chosen."

Yeshua stared at the blood-red wine of the third cup. He absently lifted a piece of bread, then dropped it, the actions of a man so deep in thought he had little conscious realization of what his hands did.

"But this is to bring about what the Scripture said," Yeshua said, lifting his eyes to those around the table again. "'The man who ate at my table has turned against me.'"

Peter lost himself to his impulsiveness and strong nature. The very thought that a man might share a meal with a host then behave in any traitorous manner was so vile to the honor code of society that Peter opened his mouth to protest. And to think Yeshua believed this so strongly he referred to it a second time.

Yeshua cut Peter's protest short with a quick shake of the head. "I am telling you now before it happens so that when it happens, you will believe that I am he."

He paused. Although Yeshua's next statement made little sense to Peter when he first heard it, he later understood it was meant to contrast with the actions of the betrayer. "I tell you the truth, whoever accepts anyone I send also accepts me. And whoever accepts me also accepts the One who sent me."

Yeshua's shoulders slumped. His face softened in sad defeat. He knew the future. He already felt the pain of betrayal. "I tell you the truth, one of you will turn against me."

The repeated emphasis of this predicted betrayal threw the table conversation into excited disarray.

Peter, directly across from John, motioned for his friend to lean forward.

"Ask him which one he means," Peter said.

John nodded and leaned back against Yeshua.

"Lord, who is it?" John asked in a low voice.

Yeshua had begun to assemble a sop of unleavened bread wrapped around bitter herbs and meat from the Passover lamb.

"I will dip this bread into the dish. The man I give it to is the man who will turn against me."

Yeshua dipped the sop into a sauce of stewed fruit, and handed it to Judas.

Obvious as the message was, John did not understand it. Judas was in the place of honor, and so would be expected to receive the first sop.

Before John could ask Yeshua to clarify his answer, Yeshua dipped another piece of bread into the dish of sauce and handed it to the disciple beside Judas.

John gave Peter a silent shrug to indicate that the master had not really answered.

Yeshua began to dip more bread, and, although he did not speak loudly, John overheard.

"The thing that you will do," Yeshua said to Judas, "do it quickly."

John misunderstood the second time, so inconceivable was it that Judas—the one who worked hardest, the one trusted with the money—might be the betrayer. Yeshua, it seemed, was sending Judas on an errand to buy something for the Passover feast or to give something to the poor.

Judas Iscariot, bread from his master still in hand, rose and departed into the night.

39

I spent most of my wait at the palace in a shadowed corner of an opulent hall. Other men arrived; as they talked among themselves, I had the opportunity to find solitude with short strolls into the courtyard beyond.

Naturally, my thoughts turned to the man of miracles. I wondered whether a meeting with him would have changed the course of my plans. What if I had found him the day before? What if he had promised to heal my daughter? Would I now be frantically running through the city, trying to find and warn him? Would I have used my wealth to offer him safe escape? And would I now feel this utterly lonely, counting down the dark hours to my final day?

But I had not found him the day before. He had not promised to heal my daughter. And somewhere in the city, a man was slipping through the dark streets to come to the palace and earn thirty pieces of silver.

When Judas left, the slight wrinkles of worry around Yeshua's eyes disappeared. Surfacing to replace that tension was his love for the men who had stayed with him through all the troubles of the previous months.

The disciples slowly ate the sop Yeshua had given them. In the lamp light, the juice of the roasted lamb shone off their lips and the edges of their beards.

"Now the Son of Man receives his glory, and God receives glory through him," Yeshua told them. He alone was not eating. His arms rested lightly on the table. His hands were relaxed and open. "If God receives glory through him, then God will give glory to the Son through himself. And God will give him glory quickly."

Every man around the table had been raised in the Jewish tradition, taught in Jewish synagogues. Every fiber of their conscious beings, all their collective understanding of religion, should have recoiled at the blasphemy coming from Yeshua. Yet a great power was descending upon them, opening their hearts to understand the mystery in Yeshua's words.

They heard, too, the affection as he continued to speak.

"My children, I will be with you only a little longer. You will look for me, and what I told the Jews, I tell you now: Where I am going you cannot come."

Peter set down his food, ready to disagree with Yeshua.

Yeshua smiled, reading his mind. "I give you a new command," he said, slipping into the role of teacher. "Love each other. You must love each other as I have loved you. All people will know that you are my followers if you love each other."

He paused to give emphasis. "If you love each other."

Peter broke into Yeshua's discourse. "Lord, where are you going?"

Yeshua smiled again. Indeed, he had known where Peter's impetuousness would lead. "Where I am going, you cannot follow now."

Peter brought his arms up, his usual preliminary to the hand waving that accompanied his passionate speeches.

Yeshua forestalled Peter's obvious reply by adding, "But you will follow later."

"Lord, why can't I follow you now?" Peter asked.

Yeshua lost his gentle smile as his lips tightened in a grimace of pain. He shook his head. "Are you ready to die for me?"

Peter nodded vigorously.

"I tell you the truth," Yeshua said, "before the rooster crows, you will say three times that you don't know me."

Yeshua took the remaining unleavened cakes of bread. He began to break them as part of the ritual to end the Passover meal. He gave a prayer of thanks and raised the bread to all the disciples. "This is my body, which I am giving for you. Do this to remember me."

This unexpected break from the usual words of the Passover ceremony and the strangeness of the command deflected all attention from Yeshua's somber prediction for Peter.

Yeshua continued, filling the third cup of wine, the traditional close to the Passover supper. He spoke as if confident that now, or later, these followers would understand the symbolism; the outward elements of bread and wine were to a man's body what the act of accepting each in Yeshua's memory was to his soul. Physical nourishment. Spiritual nourishment.

"This is my blood which is the new agreement that God makes with his people. This blood is poured out for many," he said to them. "I tell you the truth, I will not drink of this fruit of the vine again until that day when I drink it new in the kingdom of God."

Because the disciples were quiet in their efforts to grasp his words as they passed and shared the wine, Yeshua tried to reach out to them.

"Don't let your hearts be troubled," he said, first looking at John. "Trust in God, and trust in me."

Yeshua waited until John gave him a tentative smile. Then he turned to the next disciple.

"I would not tell you this if it were not true." Again, Yeshua looked into the eyes of his disciple. He waited until the man's heart heard the call of God before moving on to search the eyes of the next.

"I am going there to prepare a place for you," he said to the next.

One by one, Yeshua soothed them, comforting them with new promises. With each new declaration, he turned to another disciple, so that those promises were not simply a long discourse.

"After I go and prepare a place for you, I will come back and take you to be with me so that you may be where I am."

To Thomas, he said. "You know the way to the place where I am going."

Thomas, conscious of Peter's earlier unanswered question, refused to accept the comfort of Yeshua's gaze. "Lord, we *don't* know where you are going. So how can we know the way?"

By then, the cup had been passed all around the table. Yeshua took it from John, set it down, and turned back to Thomas to answer him directly. "I am the way, and the truth, and the life. The only way to the Father is through me."

Yeshua spoke to the others, almost as an appeal. "If you really knew me, you would know my Father too."

The knowledge of the night's future clouded his face, and

Yeshua spoke more softly. "But now you do know him, and you have seen him."

Philip broke the mood. "Lord, show us the Father. That is all we need."

What could have gone through Yeshua's mind? So close to the end of his earthly time with them, and at this moment so close to heaven that surely the awareness of God was reaching their souls, illuminating the prisons of their frail mortal bodies. Yet Philip still insisted on clinging to the pitiful limitations of his external senses, as if Yeshua were offering them the actual sight of God to quell their doubts and fears, when faith alone gave spiritual vision.

"I have been with you a long time now. Do you still not know me, Philip?" Yeshua asked.

He addressed all the others. "Whoever has seen me has seen the Father. So why do you say, 'Show us the Father'? Don't you believe that I am in the Father and the Father is in me?"

They appeared frightened. At his exasperation? At the force of his words? At the almost inconceivable notion of the God of the universe sitting among them? At the overwhelming shift of perception a man must make if he acknowledged with heart and soul and mind that God had become man?

Yeshua softened, unable to avoid his compassion for them. "The words I say to you don't come from me, but the Father lives in me and does his own work. Believe me when I say that I am in the Father and the Father is in me."

He paused to think, as if searching for a way to set these fledglings free from the pull of gravity and linear time—a way to help them understand there was One who superseded nature in the very act of creating it, One intent on opening their wings for flight through the eternity they could not see beyond their short lives.

When Yeshua was ready, he spoke so softly they had to lean forward to hear. "Or believe," he finally said, "because of the miracles I have done."

There it was. As plainly said as possible. If they were only able to view the world from the bodies of men—not with the eyes of their eternal souls someday destined to be free—then it should be enough that they had seen Yeshua shape events in the natural world with a power from beyond it. As, too, it should be enough for anyone who later heard witness of his miracles.

There it was. He was a lunatic. Or he was God.

And too soon, they—like every generation to follow— would only have the memory of his short time on earth to make that choice.

40

Hindsight can provide piercing, and sometimes regretful, clarity.

But regarding Judas, a backward look offers only his actions; his mind is curtained by his silent grave. My own guess—and it is merely a guess, no better or worse than any other I have heard since that night—was that Judas fell prey to the talent given him at birth.

Our greatest temptations generally arise from the areas closest to our hearts. A man with no weakness for food cannot become a glutton; neither can a lazy, unambitious man be tempted by power. As Judas was the keeper of the purse, we can guess at his administrative skills and a sharpness with money, two ingredients for ambition. That he was trusted during Jesus' entire ministry shows the others thought highly of him; engaged in what suited him, he was likely content for most of his time with the prophet.

Yet behind this aptitude he probably had—as we all do—a darker side. Once his ambition was thwarted, honesty too easily soured to dishonesty; ideals decayed to disillusionment; service became frustration, resentment, and thoughts of betrayal.

Until finally, these thoughts became action.

When Judas arrived, I happened to be near a decorative imitation marble panel at the rear of the hall. It was the fashion these days, and I had made considerable profit shipping and selling the deep, rich pigments to mix into plaster.

My pretended intense admiration of the workmanship allowed me to avoid conversation with those around me, and only their sudden collective silence alerted me to Judas's presence. I simply turned and saw him, a slim man with an even-featured, handsome face bearing a well-trimmed beard, eyes distorted with the shine of desperation.

His voice broke as he promised to lead us to the chamber where the prophet celebrated Passover with the remaining disciples.

My first impression of him—and the others' reaction to him—brought to my mind a picture of a dog slinking sideways as it approached its master, uncertain of reward or punishment.

Judas received only grunts of acknowledgment for his information along with disdain, obvious in the curl of lips and the shaded looks down noses.

I think I understood why everyone disliked him. The obvious reason was that his presence served as a reminder of the shamefulness of hating a man who rightfully reminded all of their failings.

I believe, however, there was more.

In the heated passion of ideological disagreement, men can accept, even admire, another who is compelled to such a defined act as betrayal for a greater cause. But all found it repugnant that Judas had requested money for his betrayal, and more repugnant that Judas had agreed to the legal price of a slave for his deed.

(I've often wondered if this price was offered so they could later balm their consciences by telling themselves they had purchased Yeshua like any other slave, giving some sort of mock ownership that would allow them to legally hand him over to the Roman authorities.)

Thirty pieces of silver.

At this price, Judas had not joined in their cause, nor had he become an associate of the powerful and elite as perhaps he had hoped.

Instead, Judas was seen as a contemptible slave trader, a hireling.

The men in the hall treated him accordingly. He was ordered to follow then ignored as their assembly moved through the night to gather armed reinforcements.

Cold high moon, pale, almost blue. Stars shivered in a blanket of black. Dim square outlines, houses crammed together in poverty. Temple gates shut.

A small group of men—once thirteen, now twelve—crossed the south plaza, the shuffling of their footsteps a broken cadence of retreat. Ahead of them stood the city gates leading into the Kidron Valley—behind them, a city stilled in solemn observance of religious ritual.

The remaining eleven disciples had no sense of the events ahead, no sense that their beloved teacher would truly die before the next sunset. Later they would look back and understand that Yeshua knew his future as he led them from the upper city through the narrow dark streets of Jerusalem. He had abandoned the teaching style of parables and spoken quietly to them in plain words of the world beyond the body, promising a Spirit to comfort them in his absence.

Yet clearly as he spoke, Thomas and Philip struggled to understand. Midway across the plaza, and near the back of the group, Philip, afraid of being chastised again, leaned over to Thomas and whispered his question. "What does Yeshua mean when he says, 'After a little while you will not see me, and then after a little while you will see me again'?"

Thomas shook his head.

Philip whispered again. "What does he mean when he says, 'Because I am going to the Father'?"

Yeshua could not have overheard. Philip and Thomas knew that without doubt. Yet, Yeshua broke off his teaching to answer Philip. "Are you asking each other what I meant when I said, 'After a little while you will not see me, and then after a little while you will see me again'? I tell you the truth, you will cry and be sad, but the world will be happy. You will be sad, but your sadness will become joy. When a woman gives birth to a baby, she has pain, because her time has come. But when her baby is born, she forgets the pain, because she is so happy that a child has been born into the world. It is the same with you. Now you are sad, but I will see you again and you will be happy, and no one will take away your joy."

None understood, and a gloom seemed to fall on them.

Yeshua turned away from them and continued his slow, steady walk toward the darkness beyond the city. The others followed.

41

I stamped my feet and shivered, as did many of the men milling around me. We stood at the gate at Antonia, the square stone fortress that butted against the northwest corner of the temple walls. Its ramparts overlooked the courts. Intimidating in height and bulk, it was still a poor second to the temple itself. The temple, however, did not have a moat. Nor did the temple hold six hundred Roman soldiers, assembled to keep the peace during Passover.

Antonia, of course, had both.

Armed only with torches, we had been a quiet procession crossing the bridge over the moat. The light of our flames bounced off the placid water beneath us. A sentry had seen us, and when we arrived at the gate, it was a simple task to send a message to the captain, who hurried out for a quick consultation with Caiaphas.

I overheard only snatches of their conversation, enough to understand that the captain was unsure of procedure, which was what forced our wait in the cool night air.

When the captain finally returned, he announced that we should follow him and the soldiers to Herod's Palace, so named because it once belonged to Herod the Great. Roman governors, as Pontius Pilate, used it as residence when in

Jerusalem. Herod, Tetrarch of Galilee and beheader of John the Baptist, made his Jerusalem quarters the Maccabean Palace, near the chief priest's palace. We would not proceed this night without permission from Pilate.

About sixty soldiers escorted us back through the city, armed with swords and shields. Volunteers and onlookers joined us as we walked. By the time this group reached Herod's Palace, there might have been as many as a hundred and fifty people.

Later, when I had a chance to make more sense of this hurried night, I would realize the herald who disturbed Pilate's sleep also woke his wife, Procula. For her, the sight of so many men gathered on the street beneath the palace balcony must have been a disturbing sight; Pilate's previous miscalculations had resulted in other night mobs howling loud protest, and our torches flickering up at her would only remind her of those earlier times. Thus, it came as no surprise when I later heard that bad dreams that night inspired her to write a note of warning to Pilate as he tried Yeshua.

Having obtained Pilate's approval, the mob followed Judas as he led the soldiers to the upper room where he had left Yeshua celebrating Passover. As we walked, we could not know that Yeshua had his own agenda and, like a canny fox, had long since bolted during our delay.

At the entrance to the garden of Gethsemane, Yeshua paused. The twisted deep shadows of shrubs and olive trees, innocent in daylight, looked sinister in the countryside darkness. Yet often he and the disciples had used this garden as evening fell into night, staying for hours, sometimes until dawn. This was sanctuary, a place of peace and beauty, where the breeze caused the leaves to flutter pale gray in the moonlight, where the tall grass in the open places among the trees caressed sandaled feet that moved through it.

It wasn't fear of the garden that halted Yeshua's approach. He paused among his disciples because he faltered. He had begun to walk slowly, almost stooped with the weight of sorrow and desolation.

His voice was almost a croak. "Sit here while I go over there and pray."

Without question, all the disciples obeyed. It was usual for Yeshua to take time alone.

"Pray for strength against temptation," he said. Yeshua began to walk away, then turned back.

Had he been flooded with the cold of utter loneliness? If so, his anguish caused him to seek out the three closest to him, the men who had witnessed his transfiguration, the men who had been with him when he raised the daughter of Jairus from the dead.

Yeshua placed one hand on Peter's shoulder. With his other hand, he lightly touched James and John, the two sons of Zebedee, so that all three understood to follow. Yeshua took them on a diagonal path through Gethsemane. Well before reaching the oil press, he stopped them.

"My heart . . ." A shudder choked his words.

Arms rigid at his side, he clenched his fists and looked to heaven. The moonlight draped his shoulders and head with soft light and made visible the glistening trail of tears on his face. He drew a deep breath to find the strength to begin again.

". . . my heart is full of sorrow, to the point of death."

He turned to them. "Stay here and watch with me."

He had not begged, but the need was in his voice. The obvious agony in his soul terrified each of them. This was the man who had calmed a storm, who had walked across water. This was the man who they had dimly begun to believe might be God incarnate. What did he see that they could not? And what thing of horror could this vision be to bend him to this point of defeat?

Terror muted them.

He walked away, but not so far that they were unable to see him collapse face forward as he knelt to pray.

42

The house belonged to a widower who lived there with a son, John Mark, who was nearly grown. The widower was called out by the captain at our arrival. The man, who had dressed in haste, stood helplessly on the street before the crowd as soldiers marched inside to the upper chamber.

I noticed Judas did not accompany them. He paced nervously on the fringes of the crowd, head down, trying to ignore the stares sent his direction. Every person who had joined to swell this procession had heard, in immediate whispers, of Judas's role in this drama. By morning, it would spread rapidly among the general populace how he had betrayed the Messiah of their hopes.

I, too, watched Judas closely, idly curious at how he would react when Yeshua appeared as the soldiers' captive.

But the soldiers returned almost immediately, without Yeshua.

Caiaphas screamed at them to search the house. They ignored him, waiting for an order from the captain, who sighed and told them to go through all the rooms.

Again they returned without Yeshua.

Caiaphas stepped close to Judas.

"You make us look like fools," he snarled. "Where is he?"

The torch light threw dancing shadows across Judas as he screwed his eyes shut to think.

"There is only one place he would be at this hour," Judas said. "In a garden. It is called Gethsemane."

As Yeshua prayed a stone's throw away, there was no one to explain to the three who sat against the trunk of an olive tree.

A man is born with the seal of death's claim already stamped on his soul. Body and soul are fused from the beginning to be torn apart at the end, this dissolution a mystery so unknowable that every instinct and every breath fights against the moment of death and the soul's rebirth beyond.

To One born into this world without the taint of death upon his soul, without the lifelong struggle of flesh dimming the spirit's awareness of God, the approaching dissolution of body and soul held not fear, but the ultimate loneliness of being caught between God and man, unable to take comfort from either side.

Yeshua, in the conflict the men could not share, prayed aloud, and his voice carried to the three.

"My Father, if it is possible, do not give me this cup of suffering. But do what you want, not what I want."

Born only of flesh, Peter and the two sons of Zebedee could only hear, not understand, the prayer uttered by Yeshua.

Through Yeshua's prayer, body and soul cried out to God. Both agonized in the contradiction of a perfect duality submitting to the humiliation of death. It was the spiritual anguish of a single star shrinking to oblivion in an eternal midnight of infinite black. And a physiological anguish so great that the body responded by squeezing the vessels near the skin into a bloody sweat.

Drops of blood fell from Yeshua's brow, marking the grass with the scent that drew the stalking presence of the hunter Satan.

We marched through the city and into the countryside. Some of the soldiers carried torches set on high poles, casting light far and wide to aid their search.

I wondered if I should try to slip away and circle ahead, out of range of the torch light. If Yeshua was ahead, I could warn him. Even now in my disbelief, I still held that remnant of hope—and perhaps in his gratitude he would help my daughter.

Or perhaps once we arrived, I could help him escape among the confusion of so many men.

It was a thought. I held on to it as we proceeded deeper into the countryside.

Where his soul's agony led Yeshua to deep and passionate prayer, inexplicable dread settled on Peter and the two sons of Zebedee like a heavy blanket, and their stress-fatigued bodies escaped into sleep.

Utterly alone in the garden, Yeshua returned for comfort to the three men who knew him best and found them oblivious to his suffering.

"You men could not stay awake with me for one hour?" he asked Peter. "Stay awake and pray for strength against temptation."

He admonished them gently, for to him they were children

in need of compassion. "The spirit wants to do what is right, but the body is weak."

Yeshua again left them. The hunter waited in the shadows beyond to wrestle with his soul.

I was near Caiaphas when the Roman captain stopped him. "This man you seek," the captain said. "How will we know him?"

Perhaps Judas was anxious to redeem himself. More than a hundred men were walking along a country road at night because of him. And what if he were wrong about the whereabouts of Yeshua? Fool would be added to the name betrayer.

Thus, Judas anxiously answered before Caiaphas spoke.

"There will be no mistake, " Judas said. "I will greet him with a kiss."

At Yeshua's second departure, Peter and the sons of Zebedee had tried to straighten to alertness. The hard coldness of the ground and the nip of the night air should have been ample discomfort to keep them awake.

But a palpable presence of evil in the garden pushed them down, so that in utter weariness they were already sinking as Yeshua's renewed prayer reached through the fog of heaviness on their eyes.

"My Father," he cried, "if it is not possible for this painful thing to be taken from me, and if I must do it, I pray that what you want will be done."

None knew how much time had passed before Yeshua's second return for comfort and companionship.

He found them in slumber, and stood over them, smiling sadly at the peace of their sleep.

Peter stirred, dimly aware of Yeshua's presence. But Peter's sleep was so deep he could not rouse himself.

Peter dropped into unconsciousness again as Yeshua stepped back into the darkness for a final savage, silent battle with the hunter.

We were almost at the garden. I told myself I did not care about the prophet's fate.

I was lying to myself, of course. Otherwise I wouldn't have been among the mob arriving to take him captive.

Part of me perversely hoped he was not the Messiah, but a fraud.

I could not deny, however, that more of me hoped for another miracle.

Dozens of torches lit the approach to Gethsemane's low garden walls, throwing warning flares of brightness that reached like fingers through the trees where Yeshua finished his prayer.

Without hurry, he moved to Peter and John and James. He crouched beside them and gently shook each one to wakefulness. Peter's hair had fallen over his eyes, and Yeshua softly pushed it away for him.

"Are you still sleeping and resting?" Not a question with the base of anger, but more like a father, upon finding his children asleep in the corner of a host's house, waking them to carry them home.

As the men blinked and yawned, Yeshua pointed at the bobbing light of the torches, now almost at Gethsemane's entrance where the other eight disciples waited.

Yeshua said, "The time has come for the Son of Man to be handed over to sinful people."

Groggy, they didn't quite understand.

"Get up!" he commanded. "We must go."

They stood and lurched on uncertain legs as they followed him through the trees, not fleeing but instead going forth to meet the mob.

In the darkness, even with the torch light, it was hard to distinguish how many men approached. It was clear, however, by glimpses of swords and clubs and armor that among them were Roman soldiers.

The other eight disciples were huddled in a nervous group, waiting for Yeshua. He stepped through them, calming them with low words.

While they peered through the confusion of the darkness, Yeshua spoke, for his vision was different from theirs.

"Look, here comes the man who has turned against me."

And Judas and the soldiers stepped through the garden entrance.

43

Judas broke away from the crowd and quickly crossed the short gap to reach Yeshua and the disciples behind him. Illuminated from behind by the torches, to the other eleven Judas was just a dark figure detaching itself from other shadows. He, however, had no difficulty discerning the features of the men who awaited him. With unerring line, he reached Yeshua.

Raising both hands in enthusiasm, Judas called loudly. "Greetings, Teacher!"

He brought a hand down on each of Yeshua's shoulders and hugged him closely, kissing first one side of Yeshua's face, then the other.

"Judas, are you using the kiss to give the Son of Man to his enemies?" It was a sad question that needed no answer. Judas had expected Yeshua to react with anger or shock. Either would have given him great satisfaction. Either would have allowed Judas to spill his bitterness and tell Yeshua he had been a fool to forsake the chance of becoming the Messiah and conquering the Romans, and an equal fool to slight Judas in as many ways as he had. It would have allowed Judas to remind Yeshua of all that he had sacrificed and how he had worked hardest of the followers to please Yeshua. And for what, he had been prepared to ask with proper indignity. All this would have given Judas justification for the kiss of betrayal.

Instead, Yeshua's resignation became a heart blow to Judas. In one horrifying moment, he realized the full magnitude of what he had done—feeling the desperate shame of a straying husband who, before the sin, had enjoyed the intoxicating temptation and the shivers of false expectations, only to see clearly after the sin the pain he had caused his wife.

Judas, are you using the kiss to give the Son of Man to his enemies?

Would that he could have turned and sent the soldiers and the chief priests away. Would that he could have fallen at Yeshua's feet and begged for forgiveness. Would that it could have been any other moment along any of the dusty Galilean roads when the sun shone brightly and the future was filled with the hope that Judas had first carried in the presence of Yeshua.

But behind milled the mob that Judas had led to his master's garden. Much as black remorse overwhelmed him, Judas could not turn back.

"Friend," Yeshua said, "do what you came to do."

Judas was too stricken to reply.

I had been considering without much seriousness whether to try to help the prophet.

It wasn't Pascal's insistence that I be seen as Yeshua's foe that stopped me from action. I did not care how my reputation might suffer among these Pharisees and Sadducees and curiosity seekers. As with possessions, a reputation is only worth something to a man when he is alive.

Instead, I held myself back because of logic. Pascal had persuaded me to accompany Caiaphas by telling me it was a way to prove—or disprove—the messiahship of the man of miracles.

I still wanted proof.

So I would watch.

If he failed to rescue himself, I would know he was a fraud.

If the miracle occurred and he saved himself from these soldiers, I wanted to stay within following distance. When the first opportunity presented itself, I would approach him.

Yes, it was cowardly of me. But I was far beyond worrying about my own opinion of myself.

The Roman soldiers neared Judas and his teacher. Yeshua stepped around the betrayer to challenge the crowd.

As the soldiers arrived, Yeshua asked, "Who is it you are looking for?"

"Yeshua from Nazareth." The reply came from one with the bravado and contempt of a bully soldier facing an unarmed civilian.

"I am he," Yeshua said.

His calm regal assurance was uncanny to the soldiers. This was not a man frightened by the full authority of the Roman empire but one who acted as if he, not they, controlled the situation. A man, then, who might have actually performed the rumored miracles that had reached their ears in the fortress above the temple. Their instinctive reaction was a superstitious fear of some magical retribution, and the soldiers closest to Yeshua stepped back and stumbled on the feet of the soldiers directly behind. More than a few tripped and fell to the ground.

Swords and shields clanked as soldiers scrambled to their feet. The rest of the mob had begun to press in, and there was no place for the soldiers to flee.

"Who is it you are looking for?" Yeshua asked again.

"Yeshua of Nazareth." This time, the answer was respectful.

"I told you that I am he," Yeshua said. He swung his right arm to point at the disciples behind him. "So if you are looking for me, let the others go."

Lightning had not struck. No ghosts or demons had appeared. The soldiers' fear passed, and Yeshua's reminder of the other eleven men snapped the centurion from his brief paralyzation. His military mind assessed the immediate possible danger; if the eleven men rushed them, fighting would be difficult in the crowd. A Roman sword could easily strike one of the chief priests. Such a political disaster would end his career.

"Now!" the centurion barked. Once they held Yeshua, the others would not dare attack. "Seize him!"

In the milling confusion of figures and shadows in flickering torch lights, Peter moved to the edge of the mob, surreptitiously withdrawing his short sword from his clothing. It would have been suicide to attack one of the armed soldiers, and equally suicidal to injure anyone with the political standing of chief priest, so he moved toward one of the servants.

He did not want his defense to go unnoticed by Yeshua. Judas, who had taken the place of honor, had betrayed Yeshua. Peter, forced into the seat of least honor, would do the opposite.

"Lord!" Peter shouted as he swung. "Should we strike them with our swords?"

Peter's target jumped sideways at his warning cry, and the

sword sliced along the servant's skull, shearing off part of his ear.

"Stop! No more of this!" Yeshua commanded. Although a soldier was about to grab Yeshua, he stepped away unhindered. None made a move to stop him as he reached the whimpering servant.

Yeshua put his left arm around the servant's slight shoulders to comfort him. With his right hand, he touched the man's ear. When Yeshua pulled his hand away to examine it in the torch light, he saw blood.

"Put your sword back in its place," he said to Peter. "All who use swords will be killed with swords."

Yeshua's irritation was obvious. That Peter had swung at a defenseless man instead of a soldier spoke plainly of the act's true meaning. And did Peter not yet understand that Yeshua was not here to establish a kingdom on earth?

"Surely you know I could ask my Father," he snapped at Peter, "and he would give me more than twelve armies of angels."

Quick as the irritation had struck, it left. Yeshua allowed that Peter still needed instruction, as did all children. "But it must happen this way to bring about what the Scriptures say."

As calmly as he had stepped away from the arresting soldiers, Yeshua returned to them. Because all attention was on him, none immediately noticed the servant he had left behind, who was touching his ear in great wonder, amazed that the bleeding and pain had ended.

The appearance of resistance had been enough for the centurion. He commanded the soldiers nearest him to immediately bind Yeshua.

Other soldiers moved to capture the disciples, but they fled into the shadows of the trees. One, John Mark, the son of the man who had given the use of his house for Yeshua's Passover, twisted in the hands of a soldier and spun away only by slipping through his outer garment, expensive fine linen instead of the usual wool. That he had dressed in haste was obvious by the flashes of pale flesh that showed his nakedness as he ran.

A soldier began chase.

"We have who we need!" barked the centurion. "Return and regroup!"

The last thing he wanted was to have his soldiers running around in the confusion of the dark grove beyond the torch lights. He'd seen night battles where Romans actually attacked Romans, such was the adrenaline and panic of men fighting for their lives.

The soldiers returned as the ropes were tightened around Yeshua's wrists.

Yeshua looked over the soldiers at the chief priests and their servants.

"You came out here with swords and clubs as though I were a criminal. I was with you every day in the temple, and you didn't arrest me there. But this is your time—the time when darkness rules."

THURSDAY NIGHT

44

I remained with the soldiers and the priests and the captive. I knew I would not sleep anyway in the solitude of my cousin's guest chamber. And, because I had watched the captive heal the lame—unless it had been fraud—I still believed there was the smallest chance the man of miracles was biding his time, waiting for the moment when messianic drama would be its most impressive to the largest number of spectators.

The walk back from Gethsemane was hardly more than a mile. But uphill, at night, and with Yeshua stumbling at the prodding spears of soldiers, it took close to an hour to reach the gates that led to the courtyards of the high priest's palace.

Well behind us, John and Peter watched. They had not run far from the garden, and while their devotion did not extend to sharing captivity with their master, neither could they completely abandon him. . . .

"They know me there," John said, pointing at the crowd as it disappeared through the gates. "My father does business with that family. I'll go in and find out what I can."

Peter nodded, dumb with fright and cold. He wanted to

flee, yet was drawn to stay with Yeshua. His helplessness and uncertainty made him miserable.

He hung back while John walked ahead.

A cassocked priest passed by Peter, accompanied by a servant to guard him in the late night.

At the gate, John spoke briefly with a woman servant, and she opened it for him.

Peter stamped his feet, crossed his arms, and jammed his hands in his armpits for warmth. As the wait lengthened, more and more men began to pass him on the street, heading to the palace gate like dark, silent bats converging on a cave's entrance.

The call had gone out. Yeshua was captured. Those of the leading priests, elders, Sanhedrists, and Pharisees who had not been part of the arrest were assembling to cast judgment on the carpenter from Galilee.

I had lost sight of Yeshua among the servants and soldiers and men of religion. More and more men arrived, so I assumed Yeshua was still somewhere within the palace. I had no worry that I was missing anything of significance; as all of these arriving men remained in the courtyard where I waited, it was doubtful that he was being tried.

At least not by the Jewish Sanhedrin. Not yet.

Annas, the former high priest, sat on an ornate chair in an inner chamber of his son-in-law's palace. Beside him stood a personal attendant with the build and face of a gladiator. He had been a wonderful find; in the course of business, Annas often rankled others and found it convenient to have the protective cloak of the man's intimidating presence.

Annas had been expecting the soldiers to arrive first. When they brought Yeshua to the inner chamber, he instructed them to wait outside the door. Because of the influence Annas had with Pilate, the soldiers obeyed without question.

When the door closed behind them, Annas examined Yeshua with the cynical eye of an experienced slave trader.

"Somehow, I expected more," Annas said. "At your touch, the lame walk and the blind see. Or so I have heard."

Yeshua, hands still bound, gazed back at Annas without shame.

Annas lifted his tunic to expose his gnarled legs. He pointed at his knee. "I have an ache when I walk. Will you heal it for me?"

No nod. No shake of the head from Yeshua. Just calm dignity.

"Truthfully," Annas said, "I admit to some curiosity. Show me a miracle, and I will do my best to save you from my son-in-law's hatred. Indeed, perhaps we can join forces. With the reach of my influence, we could both profit magnificently."

Yeshua closed his eyes briefly. Then opened them. Still silent.

"You cannot speak?" Annas asked. He dropped his tunic, suddenly embarrassed at his exposure. "Is it from shock that we have finally acted?"

Silence.

Annas curled his lips in a smile of derision. "I think of a monkey, throwing sticks at an elephant, running up and down its back, shouting high-pitched taunts. It grows bolder and bolder because the elephant does not respond. And then, suddenly, the great beast swings around and grabs the monkey with its trunk."

Annas laughed at Yeshua's continued silence.

"And as the elephant shakes the monkey in the air," he went on, "the monkey discovers how insignificant it is and how powerful the beast it thought it could tame."

Yeshua merely kept his eyes intently on Annas's face. The strength in his silence unnerved Annas.

"Jibber, jibber, jibber," Annas continued, unaware of the irony of his own taunting against Yeshua's stoicism. "The monkey goes jibber, jibber, jibber until the elephant snatches it and squeezes it. And the monkey dies."

Still no response.

Annas would never have admitted it to himself, but Yeshua's dignified silence had become a power of its own. So, trying to establish his superiority, Annas leaned forward and pressed his interrogation. "Tell me, are there other little monkeys to throw themselves at the elephant?"

Yeshua maintained his calm gaze.

"Let me translate for your provincial mind," Annas said, making his scorn obvious. "How many followers do you have? Do they contribute money to support your cause? Are they armed?"

Annas had hoped he could anger Yeshua and, in so doing, trick him into incriminating his disciples.

Yeshua smiled peacefully. He could have answered that a judge attempting to extort confessions to which he had no right was not a fair inquiry.

"And your teachings," Annas demanded, moving on so that the continued silence was not a victory for Yeshua. "What of them?"

"I have spoken openly to everyone," Yeshua said, slowly and clearly. "I have always taught in synagogues and in the

temple, where all the Jews come together. I never said anything in secret. So why do you question me?"

Yeshua's simple logic caught Annas off guard. The old man
could think of no sarcastic or cutting reply.

"Ask the people who heard my teaching," Yeshua continued,
implying that if the inquiry had been fair, the judge would have
sought witnesses. "They know what I said."

It was not the craven servility that any other man would
have offered the most powerful religious authority in the
Jewish world. Annas's attendant bore it no longer.

Stepping forward and lashing out at the same time, he
swept the back of his massive hand in a crashing blow against
Yeshua's face.

"Is this the way you answer a former high priest?" he snarled.

Yeshua's top lip had cracked, and blood began to film his
teeth. When he spoke, however, his calm patience concealed
any pain. "If I said something wrong, then show what it was.
But if what I said is true, why do you hit me?"

It was enough for Annas. The superiority he had first felt in
front of Yeshua had disappeared. He did not see any way to
regain the upper ground against this man, and that realization,
too, was further defeat. He was beginning to understand why
Caiaphas had such a hatred for this carpenter from Galilee.

"If this man will not answer questions," Annas said, "this
hearing is finished."

He did his best to affect an air of boredom as the soldiers
reentered the chamber to take Yeshua away.

Dozens of men had passed Peter, and, seeking the safety of
numbers, he had drifted closer to the iron bars of the gate. He

was debating whether to bluff his way past the woman at the gate when John rejoined him.

"Enough of the Sanhedrin has gathered," John said. "They are about to begin."

"Begin what?" Peter said. "I know little about the law, but enough to know any trial must take place during the day."

"Better yet," John grinned. "Much as they would like it, they can't pass a death sentence on Yeshua. It's a Roman prerogative."

He clutched Peter's arm. "Even if somehow they convinced Pilate to crucify him as our teacher predicted, there is not enough time before the Sabbath."

He began to pull Peter toward the gate. "Think of it, my friend," John said, "whatever happens in there, we will have until the new week to raise the support we need to free him. You just watch, everything will turn out right."

Peter stopped. "What if they decide to kill him themselves?"

"Sandhedrists?" John said. "Men who bind themselves with regulations? Much as they would like him dead, they won't taint themselves with something they cannot legally justify. We will have time to rally support."

Much encouraged, Peter finally returned John's grin.

It did not dampen his spirits at all when the girl at the gate gave him a hard, questioning look before she let him in with John.

45

A charcoal fire in the center of the inner courtyard threw a small glow on the bearded men as they talked in excited tones about the capture of a rebel messiah.

Peter sat among the servants at the fire and warmed his hands with them. Minutes later, he stood and began to pace. Despite the reassuring words of John, he could not calm himself.

His agitation drew the attention of the maid who had first admitted him to the courtyard.

The fire's light was uncertain, so she asked him, "Aren't you also one of that man's followers?"

Peter thought of the servants behind him. One, a cousin to the man whose ear Peter had sliced, had spoken loud and long about what he would do to the Galilean coward who had attacked an unarmed man. What might happen if these Judeans realized Peter had wielded the sword?

Peter told himself, too, that it would hurt Yeshua's case if he were brought forth as a witness to testify against him, especially in light of John's predication that they could rally support for Yeshua over the next few days. Not only that, he convinced himself, true denial would have been leaving the city instead of staying as near to Yeshua as possible.

Quick anger surged through Peter at the defensiveness he felt at her question. This was only a woman, and a servant at that. Who was she to expect Peter's answer, needless and potentially harmful as it might be?

He drew himself tall with cold indignation.

"No, I am not!" he said.

While Peter protected himself outside, I remained in the great hall with a couple dozen spectators. Naturally, I cannot say for certain what went through Caiaphas's mind, but I saw and heard enough to feel confident my witness to the record is as close to truth as anyone might offer.

The great hall in the palace of Caiaphas was not much more than an open court with an arched ceiling. Smoky torches along the walls blackened the limestone with oily resin. The light, although dim, was strong enough to give shadow outlines to the cracks of the flat, interlocked brick that formed the floor. Rows of mats had been thrown down in three semi-circles to provide seats for the council members.

Caiaphas, in his official high priest robe, stood at the side of the great hall. He watched with satisfaction as Pharisees and elders and teachers took their seats. At least twenty-three were needed for a quorum of the Great Sanhedrin; it appeared that all seventy had arrived.

Israel had three tribunals. The lowest—consisting of three judges—held limited jurisdiction, in towns with populations of fewer than one hundred and twenty men. The next highest—for larger centers—consisted of twenty-three judges, whose authority, while still somewhat limited, gave them jurisdiction over some capital causes. Finally the seventy men of the highest tribunal, Jerusalem's Great Sanhedrin, presided over all matters, and met in the temple's Chamber of Hewn Stones under the direction of the seventy-first man, the high priest, called *Nasi*, prince. There were no greater powers of authority in Israel.

As the men took their places, there was little noise beyond the rustling of clothing. Part of the silence stemmed from the lateness of the hour. As well, each man had been warned to expect the meeting, and thus knew the seriousness of the matter.

When they had seated themselves, Caiaphas strode to the front to face them. Two court scribes, also facing the tribunal, prepared to note the speeches.

"As you have heard," Caiaphas said without preamble, "the rebel has been placed under arrest. He will be brought before us shortly."

Immediately an ancient Pharisee named Jochanan, whose long bone-thin neck was wattled with loose skin, stood.

"There are legal difficulties with this," Jochanan said. His fanatic adherence to rabbinical teachings was notable, even among Pharisees. "I would like it recorded that I have made formal protest to this."

Caiaphas smiled to hide his irritation. Jochanan, in his fanaticism, hated Yeshua deeply. Which meant Jochanan was playing politics. It was his not-so-secret intent to one day act as high priest; he probably hoped this evening could also end Caiaphas's career.

"What is your protest?" Caiaphas asked.

"This trial grossly violates every tenant of Jewish law and order."

"How so, venerable judge?" Caiaphas had not risen to his position by letting challenges appear to intimidate him.

"Rabbinical law dictates that such a case as this be tried only in the regular meeting place in the temple. Furthermore, capital punishment may only be pronounced in the same place."

"Capital punishment?" Caiaphas responded. "Surely you are not suggesting—" Caiaphas bared his teeth "—that you have determined the outcome before listening to the testimony of witnesses. Such prejudicial leanings are not fitting for a Sanhedrin judge."

Jochanan gave himself time to think by losing himself in a coughing fit. When he recovered, he said, "If the *Nasi* had let me finish my sentence before reaching such a quick conclusion, the tribunal would have heard me add a simple phrase. Capital punishment—if necessary."

"Thank you for that clarification." Caiaphas bowed, reveling in Jochanan's brief humiliation. "Please continue."

"According to rabbinical law, no process of trial shall begin at night. Or even in the afternoon. Nor may trials proceed on Sabbaths or Feast Days. As the court scribe will note, it is well past midnight on the Passover, a highly unusual and unprecedented occasion for a tribunal gathering."

Caiaphas watched Jochanan's large bald head totter on his impossibly skinny neck and enjoyed the thought of hearing those bones snap. He observed the shifting and muttering of the rest of the tribunal and realized the impact of the man's words.

"Last," Jochanan said, "in all capital causes, the judges must obey an elaborate system to warn and caution any witnesses. I do not see any outside witnesses, and I wish to ask, for the record, whether normal trial procedures will be used to safeguard the accused."

Jochanan sat, smugly happy that he had trapped Caiaphas, who would lose face if he sent the tribunal home after his urgent messages to set up this night gathering. Yet if Caiaphas continued, Jochanan could sanctimoniously protest Yeshua's inevitable death sentence, keeping the moral high ground while seeing both Yeshua and Caiaphas suffer.

Caiaphas pounced immediately. He wanted the entire tribunal to realize how easily Jochanan could be outmaneuvered.

"In answer to the noted protests," Caiaphas said, smiling condescendingly at Jochanan, "this is *not* a trial, and I extend my pity to Jochanan for his inability to understand this. It is also unfortunate that he chose to waste the tribunal's time by bringing up something already known to all."

Caiaphas directed his words to the entire tribunal. "Obviously this is a matter of supreme importance. I cannot recall any other occasion that has merited the gathering of Jerusalem's religious leaders on the holy Passover night.

"Your united attendance shows, however, the great danger facing us. If Yeshua is not silenced and stirs the land to rebellion, the Romans will have every excuse to slaughter thousands of innocents and remove all authority from this tribunal. Or perhaps Jochanan has also lost the ability to understand this?"

Jochanan stared ahead stonily, knowing any answer would only add to Caiaphas's victory.

Caiaphas enjoyed letting the silence of triumph linger.

"Let me repeat," Caiaphas finally said. "This is not a trial. As learned men, we are simply gathered to determine whether Yeshua from Nazareth should be sent to Pontius Pilate for judgment."

Caiaphas gazed over the Great Sanhedrin. "Are there further comments?"

None came.

"Then we shall proceed," he said.

He motioned to attendants at the back of the hall.

They brought Yeshua forward.

46

Near the fire, one of the servants overheard Peter talking to John.

The servant cocked his ear at Peter's strong accent.

He listened a little longer, then remarked loudly, so that his observation became an accusation.

"Surely you are one of those who followed Yeshua," the servant said so others around him could hear, "because you are from Galilee too."

During his small talk with John, Peter's mind had been on the girl and his reply to her. He'd convinced himself he had done the right thing by maintaining anonymity. Peter was trapped firmly in one of the peculiarities of human nature; sometimes the more wrong a man is in his stance, the more strenuously he argues it, for a justification needs continued and further justification for the self-deception to survive.

"I do not know this man you're talking about," Peter said.

He pushed up from where he was squatting and walked away from the fire.

An hour later, it was obvious to everyone that for Caiaphas, the sweetness of victory over Jochanan had faded. His frustration stemmed from two sources. The first was rabbinical law, which dictated that two witnesses must agree to support a given charge. Caiaphas had called witness after witness to bring evidence against Yeshua. No two, however, had been able to agree on the same charge. Some had tried exaggerating or distorting different portions of Yeshua's teaching. Others had pointed to his acts of healing on the Sabbath—it was unlawful, but the politically shrewd Caiaphas had realized condemning Yeshua on that charge would also legitimize his miracles. It had reached the point where even the most ridiculous accusations were put forth, but with no results. The only thing proved by all of this was that Caiaphas had too hastily assembled the Great Sanhedrin and in his excitement had done little planning as prosecutor.

The second source of Caiaphas's frustration merely stood silently before the assembly, showing wily knowledge that it was far better to let the false and contradictory statements fall by themselves.

Caiaphas beckoned for one of the young teachers from the rear semi-circle to come forward. Caiaphas had no great hopes of them, which is why it had taken him so long to turn to the least experienced of the Sanhedrin.

"This man said, 'I can destroy the temple of God and build it again in three days.'"

Hope flared for Caiaphas, and he marked the young teacher in his mind for reward later. Any threat against the temple was blasphemy that demanded the death sentence. Properly manipulated, this testimony could prove that Yeshua was a seducer of the people, calling them to tear down the temple while promising them magical power to rebuild it. It would not necessarily hold as a capital charge in Jewish law, but Caiaphas had no intention of making this an official trial. He simply wanted something he could take to Pontius Pilate so the Roman procurator could pronounce a death sentence. And most surely, if the Sanhedrin could show Pilate that Yeshua was calling for rebellion . . .

Caiaphas called out, "Is there another witness who will testify for or against this?"

"Yes," another elder replied. "I heard him say the same."

Muted conversation rolled through the gathering. They all understood the significance of this.

The Pharisee named Nicodemus stood. "It should be brought to the attention of the tribunal that those words could be interpreted as 'the temple of the body.'"

Caiaphas glared at Nicodemus. Spies had brought word months earlier that Nicodemus had sought night-time audiences with Yeshua. Nicodemus was not raising his point as a matter of law to protect the Sanhedrin from a sentence that would not hold up under examination. Nicodemus was actually trying to protect Yeshua.

The muttering grew louder.

Caiaphas raised his voice to silence everyone. He turned to Yeshua.

"Aren't you going to answer? Don't you have something to say about their charges against you?"

But Yeshua remained silent.

Caiaphas felt his own heart pound against his ribs as his rage and hatred rose.

Yeshua, showing the wisdom of an experienced scholar, was taking advantage of the very laws they were using against him. No proven evidence had been laid forth in these hearings; legally, Yeshua did not have to reply.

"Will you not answer?" Caiaphas demanded.

All muttering stopped. The other seventy men waited. Even the scribes, who normally showed no interest in testimony, leaned forward.

Yeshua said nothing. His head was bowed down, and the swollen upper lip that distorted his face was not visible.

Attention shifted to Caiaphas as the elders and teachers of the Sanhedrin sensed a crucial point in the hearing. Unless a proven charge was introduced for their vote, the prosecution would have no case. They would have no choice but to set Yeshua free, making him even more popular with the people, and setting up extreme humiliation for the religious establishment in Jerusalem.

Caiaphas felt his composure washing away to waves of hatred and rage. It had taken him months to get this detestable peasant in his grasp.

He commanded himself to think.

Did he want to ground an accusation on Yeshua's claim to messiahship?

No! Israel's holiest and highest hope should not be exposed to mockery before the Romans.

Yet . . .

Yeshua lifted his head and smiled peacefully, as if at that moment he knew exactly what choice remained to Caiaphas.

Caiaphas wanted to destroy Yeshua because the peasant was a false prophet preaching false doctrines, because he publicly abused and ridiculed Jewish religious authority, because of the great likelihood that Yeshua would lead a popular rebellion against the Romans, and finally, because he did not deny messianic claims.

Over the last hour, Caiaphas had not been able to build a case on the first three charges. Yet the fourth charge . . .

There *was* a way to make Yeshua incriminate himself. Caiaphas would not need to find witnesses to prove and bring to Pilate Yeshua's claim to messiahship, not if Yeshua claimed it himself.

Caiaphas could find seventy witnesses! Right here!

As their eyes met through the uneven yellow light of the great hall, Caiaphas raised his right arm and pointed a long, craggy finger at Yeshua.

"I command you by the power of the living God," Caiaphas said. "Tell us if you are the Christ, the Son of God."

Somehow, the previous silence grew even heavier. The question was genius in its formulation. Once Yeshua denied it, his popular movement would cease. The Sanhedrin could set him free, to do no more damage among the people.

"Are you the Son of God?" Caiaphas demanded.

"*I am*," Yeshua said, speaking his first words of the hearing.

A near roar went through the hall as the members of the Sanhedrin absorbed Yeshua's reply.

I am.

The hallowed unspeakable phrase that only God could speak in reference to himself.

I am.

Blasphemy!

Yeshua turned to face the assembly.

"And in the future," Yeshua began, cutting short the babble, "you will see the Son of Man sitting at the right hand of God, the Powerful One, and coming on clouds in the sky."

Rabbinical law dictated that when blasphemy was spoken, the high priest rip both his outer and inner garments, tearing them so completely that neither would ever be repaired.

There was nothing judicial, however, about the manner in which Caiaphas tore his clothing. Fury animated him with passion that no elder in the assembly had ever seen him show, and Caiaphas shredded his upper garments so completely that wisps of gray hair were visible on his bony, narrow chest.

"He has spoken blasphemy!" Caiaphas shouted, releasing his months of brooding hatred. "We don't need any more witnesses! You all heard him say these things against God. What do you think?"

Starting from youngest to oldest, so that the opinions of the elders would not unfairly sway the first votes, Caiaphas asked for each man's decision.

"Guilty," the first man said. As did the second. And third. So it continued.

When the first thirty-seven members had all agreed that Yeshua was guilty of blasphemy, Caiaphas permitted himself a small smile of victory. Only a majority of two was required; with only thirty-four votes left, Yeshua's sentence had been pronounced. As Caiaphas continued polling the final votes, the only exceptions were the man named Nicodemus and another, Joseph of Arimathea, who each abstained, drawing glares from Caiaphas and whispers from the Sanhedrin.

The final count showed sixty-nine votes of guilt and two abstentions.

Technically, it had not been a trial, so Caiaphas did not pronounce a formal sentence. He would reassemble the Sanhedrin at first light at the temple for a second vote, which would legally seal the fate of the rebel.

Which, for the grave offense of blasphemy, would be death.

I waited for Yeshua to show everyone he was the Messiah. He did not.

47

They began to beat Yeshua after the mock trial; I was sickened at the joy lesser men took in trampling one they had feared.

This final injustice after the mockery of a trial I had witnessed pushed me to unreasoning anger. Perhaps I was looking for a way to vent my frustration, much as I had taken savage satisfaction in fighting the two men beneath the city earlier in the week.

Ten men had gathered around Yeshua, vying with each other to swing at him with fists or kick him.

I rushed in and tried to throw them away from him. My efforts were useless. They briefly turned their fury on me. Three men tossed me to the ground. Others kicked at me until I managed to roll away.

Two of the men made moves to pursue me, but Caiaphas stopped them. He looked down at me in scorn.

"Leave this fool," he told them. "He is the cousin of Pascal. We will hurt him as we hurt any wealthy man—by restricting his business."

I pushed to my knees and dusted myself, feeling powerless.

I knew there was now no way for Pascal to associate himself with me by purchasing my estate. And, oddly, I began to feel relief at the only alternative left to me.

When they tired of beating Yeshua, they placed him in a small room above the courtyard to pass the final hours until dawn and his sentence of death.

From there, Yeshua witnessed something that must have hurt him far more than the blows, insults, and spittle of his enemies. . . .

Peter was well to the side of the fire, conspicuous by his solitary outline. Intent on trying to overhear the results of the trial, he did not notice until too late that one of the servants had moved beside him.

The man tapped his shoulder. Although it was dark, Peter saw enough to recognize the man. It was the servant who had complained loudly about the coward with a sword.

"Didn't I see you with him in the garden?" he asked.

Before, anger had surged through Peter. Now it was fear. By the aggressive tone of the question, Peter knew he could be mobbed and beaten badly if found out.

Peter called a curse on himself to swear the truth of his words. "I don't know this man you're talking about!"

As the words left his mouth, a distant rooster crowed.

Before the rooster crows this day, you will say three times that you don't know me.

The horror of the accuracy of the prediction lifted Peter's head. He saw the one who had predicted it.

In the torch light that had illuminated the trial proceedings, it appeared to Peter that Yeshua was staring directly back at him.

Peter shoved away from the servant and stumbled in a half run, looking for any place that offered him privacy. Deep wrenching sobs overcame him.

Yeshua, too, wept.

FRIDAY

48

My dearest love,

   If our servant has read you these letters in order, you will remember easily that I would not write my final letter until I had decided the truth about this man of miracles.

   Last night I saw him captured and tried by ordinary men. Greedy men. Vain men. Self-righteous men. Men who wanted him dead because his teachings were a threat to them. Men who had the power to murder him publicly and make it appear lawful.

   For the events that transpired against him, he has my sympathy. He was innocent and, by trying to help others, condemned himself.

   Yet if he was who he claimed to be, he would not have let this injustice occur. Nor would he have taken the beatings and insults rained upon him.

   Thus I am satisfied. Altar sacrifices failed. As did fasting. Self-denial. And the pursuit of a miracle man.

   Nothing in my power will set our daughter right, or our love right, or myself right again. Knowing I have done everything possible within my considerable means and talent allows me to seek my solution in peace.

Please be assured that my beloved cousin Pascal will take care of my estate and ensure you will never want for money.

In farewell, let me tell you again that you are blameless for the death of our love. I am the one who failed. Grieve the man you remember me to be in the beginning—I beg this as my final wish. Then find a man who will cherish you until your last breath.

As I do not want my confession to reach the ears of the servant who reads this, I am writing it on a separate scroll, sealed, to be included with these letters.

Have Vashti read it to you. I know she has been seeking education; books are now her only freedom. As she reads my confession aloud in your presence, it will grant her another freedom of sorts, for she will be telling you the truth she has kept hidden from you on my behalf. Tell her my death is payment for the burden I gave her.

I ask you to forgive me if you can. Ask Vashti to forgive me. I want you both to know I would have given everything I owned to undo what I did; instead I am giving my life, and not even that is enough.

At the first star on the evening you receive these letters and the news of my death, sing a song for me from our balcony. The thought of your sweet voice will bring some happiness to me over the next few hours.

Goodbye.

49

In the prison of my cousin's guest chamber, I wrote the confession to Jaala, as promised, half expecting this act itself to somehow set me free.

It did not. In my mind, I saw my wife's face as she heard the truth. I watched her sit back slowly, absorbing what it meant. This vision of the woman I loved increased my pain.

I rolled the parchment carefully, and set it with the other letters that would be delivered to her with the possessions I had brought to Jerusalem.

I let out a deep breath of resolution. With the arrival of the dawn, my self-imposed trial had finally ended.

For another, too much trial remained. . . .

Pilate sat in his magistrate's chair, his shoulders covered with a cloak. The sun had yet to warm the courtyard, and he knew it would be another hour before he could set the cloak aside. This early hour and the judicial task that went with it was one of the reasons he disliked coming to Jerusalem.

As Roman governor, Pontius Pilate's duties included moderating all local disputes between Jews and Gentiles. Because of Jerusalem's large Gentile population, a huge backlog of cases always awaited him during his infrequent visits from

Caesarea. Pilate was also responsible for overseeing appeals, capital cases, and any political offenses that threatened Roman administration. Other duties had delayed his first hearings until Wednesday. Since then, he had held two sessions a day—dawn until noon, and midday to early evening—and still expected to be stuck in Jerusalem until the middle of the following week.

His role as provincial judge demanded full concentration. Roman courts usually had large juries, but in the provinces, because of the scarcity of Roman citizens, the governor was both jury and judge. Pilate had no room for legal sloppiness; the transcripts of all his trials were subject to review in Rome. His advancement in part depended on his reputation as a magistrate.

Pilate considered it a small mercy that the current case had required little time and even less legal skill.

He looked down on the two bearded men shivering, as much from fear as from cold, before him. Both were stripped to the waist, both mongrel thin with dozens of bruises and abrasions across their ribs; the soldiers who had captured them had not been gentle.

During a court session, there is always one totally quiet moment, the pregnant pause before the verdict is delivered. This was that moment.

As Pilate drew a breath to pronounce his deliberations, sandals scuffling over bricks broke the moment. The spectators turned to watch a slave rush into the courtyard.

The slave stopped short, seeing by the scowl on Pilate's face that it had not been a good moment to interrupt, no matter how urgent the message.

Pilate turned his attention back to the two prisoners. "The

court shall note that no less than five witnesses have described without variation your attempt at highway robbery," Pilate said. "Accordingly, I judge you both guilty."

The larger of the two men, whose nose had been broken by the butt end of a soldier's spear, urinated in a spasm of fear. He had expected the verdict, but to be in the moment when it was delivered was too much. For he also knew the penalty.

"Take them away," Pilate said. "As they are not Roman citizens, flog them first, then crucify them."

The second man bore his sentence stoically, but his wife rushed forward and tried to pull him away from the Roman soldiers. A fist knocked her to the ground, and she lay moaning in pain and misery as soldiers led the men away.

Pilate waved for more soldiers to remove her as well and sighed at the wearisome drama of human nature. He beckoned the slave forward.

"A delegation waits for you outside the palace. Sanhedrin. With the rebel."

"I have been expecting them." *Why else had they requested a cohort of soldiers in the middle of the night?* "Send them in."

"Excellency, they request you meet them outside. They wish to avoid religious defilement. If they enter now, they will be unable to participate in the remaining Passover celebrations."

"They expect me to go out to them?"

The slave hesitated.

"What is it?" Pilate said.

"Caiaphas instructed me to let you understand that he foresees dangerous rioting if this matter is not handled soon. Already, hundreds are gathering in the square outside the palace."

More hesitation.

"Out with it," Pilate snapped. When would these servants realize he was first and foremost a soldier, not a capricious emperor who vented cowardly anger on the helpless?

"I have also been instructed to let you know that their own criminal investigation has found the man guilty. Caiaphas promises this will not delay your schedule."

Pilate slammed an open palm against his chair's armrest.

"Excellency?"

Pilate was a soldier, but no soldier reached a governorship without political acumen. Much as Caiaphas wanted this Yeshua dead, he was trying to force Pilate to bear the blame for any rioting that resulted from the prophet's death. Further-more, Caiaphas expected Pilate to accept the judgment of the Sanhedrin when the very essence of Roman law was a public hearing. Any disturbances over Yeshua's death would hurt Pilate twofold in Rome: for the disturbance itself and for the legal improprieties. For Caiaphas, it was a shrewd attempt to hurt both of his enemies at the same time.

"Excellency?" the slave asked again.

Pilate realized his attention had been on his disdain for Caiaphas and his anger at the leverage of the high priest's office.

Pilate uncurled his grip on the armrest.

"Tell Caiaphas I will thoroughly judge this case."

Before the slave could move ten paces away, Pilate stood.

"Wait," Pilate commanded. He threw his cloak aside. "I have changed my mind. I will tell him myself."

50

Just before leaving the guest chamber, I took the opportunity to review, for the final time, the legal documents I had had prepared shortly before the Passover. Listed in full detail—if nothing else, I had a good head for numbers—were the total values of all my holdings.

Pascal would see this and trust me for accuracy.

Following this list was the price I had requested for the full estate, not including the villa where my wife and daughter could comfortably spend the rest of their lives if they chose. This price was only half of a conservative estimate of the estate's value, yet more than enough to allow my wife and daughter to live extravagantly each year of their lives.

Pascal would gladly pay this amount to add to his holdings.

The bargain included the provision that Pascal oversee the transfer of wealth and administer this money in such a way as to protect my wife and daughter.

My death would force Pascal to honor this deal despite my foolish actions against the Sanhedrin. And because I would be dead, none would speak against him for associating with me.

I had decided upon this as the simplest and least wearisome way to handle my holdings. I was tired of life and wanted no more burdens. If I actually entered into a discussion with

Pascal, negotiations could take days to resolve. Days I did not care to see.

I had one last note to write.

I began without hurry. In the same manner, the Roman governor began to deal with his problem in the public square not far from where I sat at my window. . . .

Pilate sent guards ahead with his magistrate's chair and orders to set it on the top of the steps, then to clear a large space in front of it.

He also sent word to Fort Antonia that reinforcements should move to the Herodian palace but position themselves out of sight of the Jews in the square.

Finally, Pilate waited fifteen minutes before marching majestically into the public square, accompanied by guards and personal slaves.

After he settled himself into the chair, he placed his forearms on its armrests.

And waited. The crowd already filled most of the square. White robes marked dozens of priests. Long gray beards indicated the Sandhedrists. Poorly dressed peasants from lower Jerusalem, some of them obviously drunk, filled out the crowd.

Pilate waited longer. Despite the impatient mutters and grumblings around him, each passing minute gave him more satisfaction. The space cleared before his chair ensured that every person would see when Caiaphas moved forward in supplication to Pilate.

The tension increased.

Caiaphas remained as stubborn as Pilate. He stood at the front of the crowd, expecting Pilate to summon him.

Pilate contented himself by examining the prisoner. There was but one man with his hands bound, so he knew it must be Yeshua. Unlike the hundreds of prisoners Pilate had seen in his career, this man's eyes held no fear, no shame, no defiance, no plea for lenience. Still—after hearing rumors of miracles for months, after seeing the efforts Caiaphas had expended to capture this prophet from Galilee, after the threats of rioting and public disorder—Pilate had expected more. A bigger man, perhaps. Or striking features. But, aside from his dignity, this man appeared as ordinary as the carpenter he'd once been.

After several more minutes, Pilate let a smile curve his lips. Enough time had passed. Caiaphas could no longer claim that Rome had not been prepared to dispense judgment. Pilate stood, smiled once more, and began to walk back toward the palace.

His bluff worked.

Excited rumblings in the crowd told Pilate that something was happening behind him. He continued to walk.

"Your excellency!"

It was Caiaphas.

Pilate pretended to hear nothing but didn't keep the gleam out of his eyes. Let Caiaphas grovel.

"Your excellency!"

Pilate sobered his features and turned back to the crowd. Caiaphas, two chief priests, and the prisoner were now at the foot of the steps, below the magistrate's chair.

Pilate resumed his position in the chair.

"What charges are you bringing against this man?" Pilate asked.

The question seemed to stun Caiaphas. Pilate's question had

been the opening formula of an official Roman trial. A nearby scribe, in fact, was copying the words for the transcript.

Pilate hid his satisfaction and amusement. Let the Jews condemn Yeshua. Let them bear the brunt of public opinion.

Caiaphas recovered badly. "If he were not a criminal," he said, "we would not have handed him over to you."

Pilate shrugged. "Take him yourselves and judge him by your own law."

The scribe continued marking Pilate's words. None of the previous night's discussion, nor Caiaphas's expectations because of that discussion, would be on the record. To any legal authority reviewing the case later in Rome, then, Pilate would be without blame.

"But we have no right to execute anyone," Caiaphas said.

Pilate nodded wisely, as if agreeing with Caiaphas. "I am to understand then, since you seek his death, that you have found this man guilty, although you have not laid charges. I am also to understand that somehow, during the night, you were able to give him a fair trial. Again, without laying charges."

A blow to the kidneys would not have had more impact. Pilate was beginning to think he had actually cornered the old gray snake before him.

Caiaphas began a heated, whispered conversation with his chief priests.

Pilate kept careful watch on Yeshua, expecting some of the conversation to visibly affect him. After all, it was *his* life at balance. Yet the prophet remained in a near meditative calm.

"We have found that this man is subverting our nation," Caiaphas announced. "He opposes payment of taxes to Caesar and claims to be Christ, a king."

Pilate waited for Yeshua to defend himself against the charges. The man said nothing. While it intrigued Pilate—defendants often shouted counteraccusations, pleaded for mercy, made excuses, but never just stood silently—it also placed Pilate in a difficult situation.

One that Caiaphas saw. For if Yeshua said nothing, Pilate would have to address the charges.

And Caiaphas took his own opportunity to smile in triumph. The three charges would alarm any Roman governor. Sedition? Opposition of tribute? The high treason of a claim to kingship?

Caiaphas knew what Pilate knew. Emperor Tiberius, in Rome, would be far less likely to understand the local situation than Pilate. Tiberius would think Pilate stupid or insane if he didn't simply and cheaply execute a non-Roman citizen to eliminate the slightest risk to Roman rule.

Pilate beckoned Caiaphas forward. He kept his voice low so that the scribe would record none of their conversation.

"I tell you this for my own satisfaction," Pilate said. "We both know this Yeshua has avoided all political causes. As for your second accusation, the nonpayment of tribute, I have had a good laugh at his now-famous response to give to Caesar what is his. You are only fortunate that what he said could be distorted in Rome."

Pilate leaned forward so he was almost nose to nose with Caiaphas. "Do you see the hypocrisy of publicly defending tribute to us when you and your Pharisees spend your days protesting Roman rule?"

Pilate's spittle flecked the high priest's beard. "And finally, it is totally contemptible that you and your Sanhedrin claim religious defilement prevents you from entering my court

246 • Sigmund Brouwer

when what you are attempting is judicial murder. Why should any man with intelligence believe you serve God?"

The only thing that held Pilate from physically pushing Caiaphas away was the certainty of the riot that would result. So Pilate stepped back and made his pronouncement.

"Send the prisoner to my chamber," Pilate said. "I will interview him there on these charges."

51

My final words, the note to Pascal, were simple. I explained that I was going to take my own life. I thanked him for his hospitality and assured him that as a younger cousin, I would have approached him for help with my problem if I had at all thought there was a solution.

I told Pascal the general area where my body might be found and asked him to keep this note secret, as it would allow my wife the comfort of a synagogue funeral if the world believed I had died at the hands of highway robbers.

I asked him to honor the document of sale he would find with the note, explaining my belief that no harm would come to his reputation if he did so after my death.

I requested that he send along the nearby letters to my wife without reading them.

Then I wrote goodbye to Seraphine and wished her and Pascal my love and shalom for the rest of their lives together.

When I discovered I had nothing else of importance to add to the note, I stood, wrapped myself in my cloak, and set the note on my bed where Pascal would find it.

I was ready to die. And I was delighted to feel a sense of calm.

As I departed the mansion of my cousin unnoticed, I pondered this calm. I decided it came to a man once he truly accepted the finality and consequences of a decision.

So, too, it must have been for the man of miracles.

"Are you the king of the Jews?" Pilate asked Yeshua.

The scratching of stylus on parchment reminded them both this was a private interview only in the sense that it was done out of the hearing of Caiaphas.

"Is that your own question," Yeshua asked, "or did others tell you about me?"

The man's utter calmness fascinated Pilate. This peasant should be quaking in the presence of the single man in Judea with the power to order soldiers into instant war against the Jewish nation.

And the man's eyes—Pilate had to harden his own soldier's heart against the gentle appeal of the prophet's compassionate gaze. *As if Pilate were the one who needed pity.*

He shook off this unexpected softness by replying brusquely to Yeshua's question. "I am not Jewish."

When Yeshua did not reply to Pilate's implication that he could not understand the Jews, the governor continued.

"It was your own people and their leading priests who handed you over to me." He pointed at Yeshua's bound wrists. "What have you done wrong?"

"My kingdom does not belong to this world," Yeshua said. "If it belonged to this world, my servants would fight so that I would not be given over to the Jews. But my kingdom is from another place."

Pilate found himself in a quicksand he had never experienced. His world was the harsh competition of soldiers and politics. As a man excelled, so his rewards increased. It was a simple world.

But, there was a subtext to this conversation, a tugging at Pilate's view of the world, that made him uneasy yet vaguely hopeful of some peace he could not define.

"So you are a king!" Pilate said, glad that the words recorded by the scribe would not contain the texture of his near helplessness.

"You are the one saying I am a king," Yeshua said. "This is why I was born and came into the world: to tell people the truth. And everyone who belongs to the truth listens to me."

Pilate felt himself sinking deeper into the quicksand. He was not a man of philosophy. Yet as he grew older, he was becoming more conscious of his mortality. There, too, was his wife, Procula, who insisted on speaking of spiritual matters, as if a man actually had a soul.

The soldier's world was simple. These other matters were not. Perhaps the world was not as simple as Pilate wished.

Here he was, the governor of Judea, a direct representative of Rome, engaged in conversation with a man persecuted by his own people for no crime that Pilate could see.

Nonsense. Any soldier would call it that. Nonsense.

Pilate also had the honesty of a simple soldier. The honesty to allow himself other questions. This near the pinnacle of his political career, what did he really have? Why did nothing really satisfy him? What was the hollowness that filled him when everything he possessed should have filled him and brought him peace?

Beyond this brief conversation and the thoughts whirling through his mind, Pilate sensed something out of his vision and touch and hearing. As if instinct were searching for a home he did not know. An instinct heightened by the man in front of him. What was it about this man? Who was this man?

A man who claimed that everyone who belonged to the truth listened to him.

Pilate set aside his confusion and went for the safety of responding cynically. He reached for the only philosophical statement he knew. Yet as the words came out of his mouth, he heard more than the cynicism he was trying to posture. Pilate heard his own half plea of hollow despair.

"You tell me," Pilate said to the man before him. "What is truth?"

52

Because I had half expected sadness as I walked through the city for the final time of my life, I defeated it before it could strike.

My face was resolutely set toward the countryside, and with the will that had vaulted me from poverty to wealth, I did not allow the sights and sounds and smells of the city to distract me from my purpose.

Perhaps I was afraid that if I looked for beauty or nostalgia, I would change my mind.

After all, I was my own executioner. If I wanted to turn back, I could.

Across the city, however, another condemned man did not have that luxury. Nor did his executioner.

Back outside the palace, Yeshua stood beside the magistrate's chair as Pilate made his announcement to the Sanhedrists.

"I find nothing against this man."

Pilate crossed his arms, defiant against the immediate uproar. He was aware of Yeshua's continued calm dignity, as if he had no fear of death.

This man was no rebel. Pilate knew it with certainty. And reflecting on their time alone in the chamber, Pilate realized how much he had revealed to the prophet, even implying a sort of homage by appealing to him with the philosophical question of truth. Was it an accident that they were standing side by side as they faced the crowd?

Caiaphas marched directly to Pilate.

"Tiberius will hear of this," he hissed above the crowd's shouting. "The letter will present a case to show the man's teachings have inflamed people from his beginnings in Galilee. Even to the point that tax collectors have followed him. And you know Tiberius and his expensive habits well enough to know how he will react to that."

Pilate only heard one word. *Galilee.*

Much as Pilate's conscience had been stirred by the presence of Yeshua, he could not escape his political nature.

Galilee.

Herod, the tetrarch of Galilee, was in Jerusalem. With diplomatic genius, Pilate could place the troublesome issue in Herod's hands and at the same time appear to be respectful of Herod's territorial claims. Perhaps Herod would see this as a conciliatory gesture in light of their current strained relations.

"It will give me satisfaction to see you recalled to Rome," Caiaphas was saying. "Most surely—"

"Take this man to Herod," Pilate said.

"Herod?" Caiaphas went from outrage to calculation.

"Herod. It is a case within his jurisdiction." Thinking it through, Pilate was satisfied. Both for how it saved him from trouble and because it would probably save the innocent man beside him. Herod would be extremely reluctant to judge Yeshua guilty. Not after the trouble he'd faced for beheading the other popular prophet, John the Baptist.

"There is ample legal right for you to preside over it yourself," Caiaphas said.

"Herod," Pilate repeated. "Your charges have religious overtones within Jewish law. He is far better qualified to judge than I am."

Pilate stood and motioned for his attendants to return the magistrate's chair to the inner courtyard of the palace. He ignored Caiaphas and gave a slight nod of acknowledgment to Yeshua as he retreated from the crowd.

As far as Pilate was concerned, there was nothing left in this affair to trouble him.

53

I did not carry a purse or valuables as I headed to the countryside. I had stripped myself of jewelry before departing.

I did not fear the possibility of bandits here on the lonely highway; rather that possibility was part of the reason I had chosen the countryside. It could have been much simpler to return to the city wall above the Kidron.

I did not know how long it would be before my body was found. But I wanted to be shorn of valuables, leaving the easy conclusion that I had been robbed and killed, discarded over a cliff.

My death must not appear self-inflicted. My beloved wife Jaala had already faced so much grief that my suicide would have little extra significance for her. But I didn't want her or my daughter to have to face questions. If others accepted my death as one at the hands of bandits, they would have no occasion to wonder or gossip about why I had killed myself. After all, to the world, I had everything.

But, as I had discovered, everything tangible can be nothing. I am certain I am not the first, nor will I be the last, to learn this. . . .

Knocking at the door roused Herod from a restless sleep. He couldn't even remember getting beneath the blankets.

"Go away," he groaned.

"Worthy Tetrarch," a voice from the other side said. "A delegation from the Sanhedrin has arrived to see you."

"Castrate each of those pompous fools and send them back to their mothers." Herod ran his tongue over his teeth and grimaced. The taste and texture were as if a small animal had crawled into his mouth and died. When, Herod asked himself, would he learn not to mix wine and beer in such great amounts?

"They insist on seeing you. It is a delegation sent from Pilate."

"Unless you leave me in peace," Herod shouted, "you will be castrated with them!"

Herod immediately regretted his foolhardy exertion. His head throbbed at the slightest movement.

"Worthy Tetrarch . . ."

Herod vowed to whip the servant himself, even if the man had served the royal family for three decades.

"Go away!" Herod tried to spit on the floor but could not work any moisture into his mouth. "No! Bring water!"

He owned an entire kingdom yet suffered hangovers like any mortal man. What justice was there in that?

"They have with them the prophet from Galilee."

Herod pushed himself upright. Blankets fell from his massive belly.

"Yeshua?" Herod asked, wobbling for balance on the side of his bed. "*That* prophet?"

"Indeed, worthy Tetrarch."

"Tell them I will see them as soon as I am ready," Herod said. "Then hurry back and help me dress."

Facing the delegation of elderly Jews from his throne, Herod wondered if their faces would crack and bleed the next time they smiled.

Arrogant, self-righteous. . . . He had half an urge to order them to stay and watch his dancers. Then he'd see just how much their rules and regulations meant to them. All except the most withered, Caiaphas, who would probably collapse with shock at the flash of the first wiggling navel.

It was Caiaphas who started to rattle off a long string of accusations against Yeshua, and his passion surprised Herod. Maybe the old man did have some life in him.

Herod listened as long as he could bear it, then waved Caiaphas to be quiet.

"Bring in your prisoner," Herod said. "I'm quite familiar with your complaints."

Too familiar. It was all these rabbis did, moan and complain. They weren't happy unless everyone around them shared their misery. Parasitic fools.

As Herod waited, he eased his throat by drinking from a goblet. *Let the fools think it's water,* he thought. But it was a hearty red wine—much needed to get his blood coursing at this early hour.

Herod's guards escorted Yeshua to the throne.

"Finally," Herod said. "I've been wanting to see you for some time."

The wine had heated Herod's veins, and he found the energy to lean forward with interest. "I have heard of your exploits for years. The great healer, you have been called. Then those stories about fish and loaves and feeding the thousands. Truly amazing. Perhaps you heard I actually sent soldiers out looking for you. But never to harm you, despite what you might have heard about John the Baptist. After all, he never performed a single miracle . . ."

All this talk scratched Herod's throat. He drank deeply and sighed. "Would you grace us with a miracle right now? Nothing spectacular. It is early, and I wouldn't want you to tax yourself too much on my behalf."

Aside from Yeshua, twenty men crowded the throne hall. Five were the limited delegation allowed. Fourteen were Herod's soldiers. And, of course, Herod.

Forty eyes stared at Yeshua. Caiaphas and the other Jews with some dread, for they feared a miracle. Herod and his soldiers with curiosity and expectation, for they hoped for a miracle.

Yeshua merely closed his eyes, as if lost in deep thought.

"Come on," Herod said. "You are here because these great religious leaders want you dead. All I need is one miracle, and you can go free."

Yeshua opened his eyes. What Herod saw in his gaze was pity.

"Listen," Herod snapped. "I'm offering you your life. Show me a sign from God, and I'll bow down before you and him. One miracle is all I need."

Yeshua only smiled sadly.

Angry, Herod gulped another mouthful of wine. "Make the rope drop from your wrists. That's all. I'll know you are a true prophet, and we'll send these Pharisees on their way."

Silence.

Caiaphas cleared his throat. "Noble Tetrarch, there is a

good reason he will not perform any miracles. He cannot. He is a false prophet. You are well within your rights to have him stoned."

Herod's headache returned with his loss of interest in Yeshua.

"Don't tell me what my rights are." He focused his irritation on the high priest. "Word of this failure will become public and the people will stop following him. He doesn't need to die to lose his power among them."

Unspoken—and both of them knew it—was Herod's fear of stirring up more trouble by killing another popular prophet.

"But he calls himself the Son of God," Caiaphas tried. "He is a heretic."

"Only an insane man would call himself such. You are to be pitied as much as him for giving his foolish claims attention."

"The Sanhedrin has found him guilty," Caiaphas said.

"Take him back to Pilate. You can continue the trial with him where you left off."

"Pilate?"

"You will notice I have not set this prophet free. Push me further and I will acquit him immediately."

Caiaphas gaped briefly, almost protested, and thought better of it.

Seeing the high priest at a loss was the first moment Herod had enjoyed since hearing the knock on his door.

Herod carefully set his goblet on the armrest of his throne. He stepped down. With two painful gout-slowed steps, he reached Yeshua.

"If you can't perform a miracle, at least talk. Let me hear you tell me you are the Son of God."

The satisfaction Herod had felt in humiliating Caiaphas

dissipated when he saw the strength in Yeshua's eyes. The knowledge and power there brought Herod's insecurities into focus through his wine-deadened senses.

"You have my apologies," Herod said sarcastically. He removed his elegant robe and draped it over Yeshua's shoulders.

"Guards," Herod called, "here is your king. Bow down. Worship him. Then take him to Pilate."

Herod's guards pounced on the opportunity for fun. They blew trumpets in Yeshua's ears. They dropped to their knees in front of him. They taunted him with vulgar comments about his ancestry.

Not once did Yeshua show any sign of discomfort. The laughter began to die.

"Enough," Herod said. "On your way."

The guards began to push Yeshua forward.

"Wait!" Herod called. As ordered, the procession stopped.

"Galilee man," Herod said, holding his goblet aloft. "Turn this water to wine!"

Herod shook the goblet as if a great force were taking hold of it. Seconds later, with the goblet a few inches above his mouth, Herod poured the remainder of the red liquid into his mouth.

"Look, look," Herod laughed. "It *has* become wine! A miracle!"

Moments later, when all had left, Herod leaned against the throne in defeat. Fat and wheezing, incapable of enjoying his wife's favors, wearying of exploring luxury and sin more with each passing year, he did not feel like a king.

How he had hoped to see a miracle. How he had hoped to believe.

54

I walked through the northern part of the city, through the Tower Gate, unaware how soon Yeshua would follow the same route. I barely noticed the houses built beyond the second wall of Jerusalem.

Bezetha, the new city, was growing rapidly past the underground quarries and the timber market, where wood was stored away from the dense inner city as a safety precaution against fire.

North, there were plateaus and small cliffs, which I had observed from the highway on my travels into or away from Jerusalem. These would suit my purpose. While I did not have a specific site in mind, I anticipated that I would know it when I saw it.

The highway was quiet. It was early on the morning after Passover. I had my solitude and my self-pity.

It wasn't until I passed the public execution site at the hill of the skull that I thought, for the first time that morning, of the man of miracles and the fate that awaited him.

Herod had sent Yeshua back to Pilate.

Because of it, the governor faced the Sanhedrists and the crowd again. Some of those gathered near the back were drunk and amusing themselves with fistfights. In the middle, hundreds of ordinary Jewish citizens—residents of Jerusalem, not pilgrims—massed together to show their support for the religious call of their leaders. At the front of the crowd, Caiaphas stood proudly and visibly among the priests and elders.

As for those who might have supported Yeshua, it was so early and this trial had convened so quickly, that none of the many who followed him even knew of the trial.

Pilate assessed the people. Yeshua's words echoed through his mind: *My kingdom does not belong to this world.*

Pilate had smelled this tension before against the fanatic Jews. It was a supercharged sweat of heated emotions, of people unified in the unreasoning passion of a mob. As Caiaphas had reminded him earlier, three other times the Jews had pushed him almost to the point of bloodshed: the riot in Caesarea, the aqueduct riot, and the removal of the golden shields. This had reached that point, and Pilate wondered if he would have to call for soldiers.

My kingdom does not belong to this world.

Pilate had first sent Yeshua away to simply thwart Caiaphas. Now, however, his determination to resist the crowd's call for the man's death came from the brief time he had spent with the prophet. His peace spoke loudly, and his single statement of defense echoed through Pilate's mind.

My kingdom does not belong to this world.

Nothing in Roman law could convict Yeshua. If Pilate took pride in any institution, it was Roman law and tradition. Aside from his unexpected admiration for the prophet, Pilate had no intention of betraying his personal convictions as a soldier and citizen of the republic.

Pilate began loudly, intending to forestall a formal trial. "You brought this man to me, saying he makes trouble among the people. But I have questioned him before you all, and I have not found him guilty of what you say. Also, Herod found nothing wrong with him; he sent him back to us. Look, he has done nothing for which he should die. So, after I punish him, I will let him go free."

Some of Caiaphas's men had been circulating near the back. They shouted as previously instructed, "Take this man away! Crucify him!"

In the shocked silence that followed Pilate's quick verdict, those shouts rang as clearly as trumpet blasts.

Within seconds, a few of the drunks took up the cry, looking to generate excitement. Their hoarse voices prompted the conservative Jews in the middle of the crowd to join.

"Crucify him! Crucify him!"

The shouts soon became a unified chant. Others, at Caiaphas's orders, had spread dissension by telling people this had become an issue of autonomy; Rome was refusing to do the bidding of Jerusalem. Still others went through the crowd, spreading the story of how Yeshua had failed to perform a miracle in front of Herod. Rage at Rome and disappointment in a failed Messiah were fueling the discontent.

Caiaphas, near the front, sat serenely, delighted that his masterful plan was working so well.

Pilate beckoned Caiaphas forward. "If a riot occurs," Pilate said in a near yell, "I hold you responsible. To keep peace, I suggest you withdraw the charges. That way I don't have to declare him innocent. As for my part, I am willing to have the man flogged to save face for you. Later, if you build a case against him that will stand up in court, bring him back to me."

Caiaphas merely backed away, smiling his contempt for Pilate. Caiaphas lifted his hands, as if accepting the orchestrated shouting of the crowd in triumphant tribute.

"Crucify him! Crucify him!"

Pilate saw a solution.

55

I left the highway and pushed my way through low brush, sweating despite the coolness of the early morning. My progress was impeded by loose sand and rocks and by the steepness of the climb.

I would not be stopped, however.

By following the empty wash of a ravine as it narrowed upward, I could reach the highest point of these hills. Then, at the top, walking along the edge of the cliff, I could see the bottom of the ravine at its widest and deepest. I would find a place where the drop was far enough and steep enough to be certain of quick death.

But certainty in this world is deceptively slippery.

Pilate knew his solution would not fail.

He had remembered a recently captured notorious insurrectionist named Barabbas. A member of the Sicarri, infamous for the short curved swords they used to assassinate Jews they marked as traitors, Barabbas had proudly confessed to killing more than twenty Jews, usually by sneaking up behind them in a crowd and stabbing them in the liver. The Romans had arrested him as he led an attempt to steal a supply train of mules.

It was the custom to release one prisoner to the Jews at Passover. Few were those who might want this killer loose among the general population.

Barabbas, of course, was the solution.

Pilate stood. Silence rippled back through the crowd, so that when he spoke, all heard him clearly.

"Whom do you want me to set free: Barabbas or Jesus who is called the Christ?"

Pilate sat again, expecting the obvious answer to the artful dilemma he had placed upon the Jews.

He might have received it, had he not attributed kingship to Yeshua by calling him "the Christ." But his reminder of Yeshua's messianic claim played directly into the anger of a crowd fanatically determined to preserve its religion by ridding themselves of a heretic.

"Barabbas!" It was a roar that surged forward. "Release Barabbas!"

Among the crowd there were a few weak shouts for the prophet, but in the confusion of the swaying mob, these people were beaten and dragged away by Caiaphas's men. No others dared to resist the outcry for Yeshua's blood.

"Barabbas! Barabbas!"

Pilate was astounded. Before he could react, however, a slave brought him a wax tablet with a message from his wife.

Have nothing to do with that innocent man, for I have suffered a great deal in a dream because of him.

It was an ominous inscription arriving at an ominous moment. The night before Caesar's assassination, Calpurnia, his third wife, had dreamed of Caesar's torn and bloody toga and had unsuccessfully tried to prevent his departure in the morning. All Romans knew of the dream, and all Romans treated dreams with respect. For Pilate, however, it was far too late to take his wife's advice.

Pilate stood. It took five minutes for the crowd to settle. Five minutes with sweat growing heavy on Pilate's face. Sweat he dared not wipe for fear of showing weakness.

When finally he could speak without yelling, Pilate asked, "So what should I do with Yeshua, the one called the Christ?"

He not only unwittingly repeated his mistake, but he had also thrown it at them with the imperial arrogance of Rome.

"Crucify him!" The roar was like an army charging forward. "Crucify him!"

Pilate looked sideways at Yeshua. The prophet was cloaked with resigned sadness but had not lost his air of deep, intense peace.

My kingdom does not belong to this world.

A soldier who reaches governorship is not bullied easily.

Pilate raised his arms and held them high until he had the crowd's silence. "Why? What wrong has he done?"

"Crucify him! Crucify him!" The shouts became more frenzied.

Pilate wondered for a moment if the mob would attack. He didn't wait to give it the opportunity. Above the deafening noise, he motioned to his soldiers to take Yeshua back inside the palace.

56

I stood at the edge of the cliff. Wind pushed against my face, its freedom mocking me.

The sky. The corner of the distant city. The red stone of the hills. All of it filled my eyes. As a last sight of the world, it was better than a sword slashing downward, or disbelief at blood pouring from a speared belly, or fevered thrashings against dirty sheets, or dark, cold water closing in, or any of a number of possible final images.

I was hopeful, too, that my death would be quick.

Eyes closed, all that remained was to dive forward into emptiness. The blue sky and red stone hills in my mind would be a balm in those final seconds. Time would have no meaning once my skull exploded against rock; there would be only nothingness.

At the whipping pillar, as the soldiers gathered around Yeshua and began to strip him, Pilate knew what to expect. During his long career, he had often been among the enlisted soldiers who engaged in the ancient custom—the games of mockery that followed after a criminal had been whipped bloody.

One soldier already held a purple robe. Another soldier had

gathered thorn branches and woven them into a crown to force upon Yeshua's head. From the vulgar banter Pilate overheard, these soldiers found it humorous that this lone, naked figure had claimed to be king. They would savage him for it and, in so doing, vent their hatred for Jews, a conquered people who refused to play the role of the conquered.

Several soldiers forced Yeshua to bend over the waist-high pillar. Runnels had been gouged into the ground below to drain blood, and flies collected on the small pools of red that lay stagnant from the earlier whippings of two convicted robbers.

A burly man stood ready on each side of the pillar, each holding a whip of leather strands woven around dozens of small shards of pottery. They waited for a signal from the governor.

Pilate told himself he was letting an innocent man be whipped for a good reason. He hoped the intense pain of the scourging would force Yeshua to defend himself against the accusations. Pilate hoped, too, that once he showed a bloody, beaten man to the crowd—especially a beaten Jew to a crowd of other Jews—a collective pity would satiate the lust for his death.

Pilate nodded.

Soldiers kicked Yeshua's legs apart to expose all parts of his body equally.

With a grunt of effort, one of the burly men swung his whip down, cracking the thongs of leather against Yeshua's back.

As he pulled the whip away, his companion aimed lower and lashed savagely from the other side. Shards of pottery raked Yeshua and curled around the inside of his thighs.

Incredibly, Yeshua did not cry out.

His silence spurred both into an enthusiastic attack of alternating whips that caused instant rivers of blood to blossom across his shoulders, ribs, and legs.

Pilate kept waiting for the man to cry out. Instead, Pilate broke first.

"Enough!" he barked.

Pilate turned his back as the soldiers swarmed in with the robe and the crown of thorns. Yet his ears could not block out the jeers of their taunts. Nor the thuds of their blows against the beaten man's face.

57

I discovered I could not do it. Standing at the edge of the cliff, I could not will myself to close my eyes and embrace death by diving forward. The spark of life burned too brightly.

I have searched myself many times since, wondering if fear or cowardice stopped me.

With all honesty, I believe it was neither.

As I closed my eyes to ready myself to jump, I could not hold the blue sky or red stone hills as my final image. Instead my daughter's face pushed its way into my mind. I saw it not defeated or in agony, but as it had been before the flames had melted the flesh of her legs: beautiful, innocent, and full of love for me. It reminded my of how much I owed because of my folly.

I finally realized that death was too easy an escape. A better punishment would be to live out my life with my daughter and her crippled, scarred legs as reminders of what I had done.

Pilate preceded Yeshua and his escort to the front of the crowd. The voices had become hoarse from shouting. Only a minority of Jews wanted Yeshua dead, but their fanaticism made up for their lack of numbers.

At the sight of Pilate, the jostling and unruliness calmed.

"Look," Pilate said, "I am bringing Yeshua out to you. I want you to know that I find nothing against him."

Pilate crossed his arms and stared at them. He did not want more of his own speech to diminish the pitiful horror of what he was about to present.

Moments later, the soldiers pushed Yeshua forward.

Pilate had guessed correctly. For a moment, no man in the crowd spoke as all strained to see the prophet from Galilee.

Yeshua was too exhausted to lift his head and face them squarely. He shivered from shock and pain. The purple robe was black with his blood. The crown of thorns had been jammed so securely on his head that more blood streamed down his cheeks and neck.

"Here is the man!" Pilate said.

Only a second passed before Caiaphas screamed, "Crucify him! Crucify him!"

It was enough to send the crowd into another frenzy. Not even Pilate's raised arms could stop it. He was forced to wait until the cries finally faded.

"Crucify him yourselves," Pilate said, directing his words at Caiaphas, "because I find nothing against him."

Pilate spoke with a finality that was clear in the set of his square face. Enough had been done to the man. Pilate intended to provide an imperial escort to take Yeshua to Galilee.

Caiaphas saw that determination.

After some hesitation, Caiaphas said, "We have a law that says he should die, because he said he is the Son of God."

Pilate felt a lurch of sliding visceral fear. *The Son of God.*

Soldier or not, he was susceptible to superstition. The uncanny peace of his prisoner, the silence of the man against all accusations. What kind of spirit ruled that man, that he would make such a claim?

Then anger displaced the lurch of fear as Pilate realized the implications of Caiaphas's statement.

Finally, forced to the wall, Caiaphas had made known the true charge held against Yeshua. It explained, too, why Herod had sent the prophet back unjudged.

"This is a new matter," Pilate snarled at Caiaphas. "I should throw the case out simply because you failed to cite this earlier. Instead, I will interview the prisoner again. In private."

"Where do you come from?" Pilate asked Yeshua.

My kingdom does not belong to this world.

Yeshua gave Pilate no answer. Blood had crusted in his beard. He stood half-crippled from torn flesh and muscles. But as always, he maintained the unearthly calm that so unnerved the Roman governor.

"You refuse to speak to me?" Pilate asked, softly. "Don't you know I have power to set you free and power to have you crucified?"

Yeshua answered, "The only power you have over me is the power given to you by God. The man who turned me in to you is guilty of a greater sin."

My kingdom does not belong to this world.

"If you had not taken away our rights to capital punishment," Caiaphas told Pilate, "you would not be faced with this problem."

They stood at the edge of the restless crowd. Yeshua was still inside the palace.

"That is the past," Pilate answered. "The man will be set free. I have no grounds to order his death."

"There will be rioting."

"Over one man?"

"You Romans never understand the Jews. This trial is not merely about a magician seducing the people with his heretical claims. Our freedom of religion is at stake. That is why the crowd is so determined to see him crucified."

"You have a stench that offends me," Pilate said. "This is about you and a battle for power. Don't try to dab perfume on a rotting carcass by claiming religious piety."

Caiaphas gave Pilate a silky smile of hatred.

"As you well know," Caiaphas answered, "your own power is slipping. You have mishandled other affairs; Tiberius Caesar is tired of disturbances in Judea. He has charged you with upholding our religious customs. If you let this man go, you are no friend of Caesar."

It was not a subtle threat.

On his index finger, Pilate wore the gold ring engraved "Caesar's friend," a symbol the emperor had bestowed before his departure from Rome. Did he want to keep the ring?

Behind Caiaphas's accusation was obvious political blackmail. If Pilate did not do as requested, the Sanhedrin could send a delegation to Tiberius with two charges against him: direct disobedience to the emperor's wish that the Jews be allowed to handle their own religious affairs, and neglect of duty for failing to punish a subversive attempting to set himself up as king.

Pilate had no place to go, unless he was willing to sacrifice his political career for a peasant.

"Do you want me to crucify your king?" Pilate asked. He was defeated, and it came out in his voice.

"The only king we have is Caesar," Caiaphas said.

Another time, Pilate might have enjoyed victory. Not only had he just heard Caiaphas pledge loyalty to Rome, but the chief religious leader of the Jews had also just denied the lordship of their almighty God.

But this was not a moment to enjoy. The crowd had begun to shout again for crucifixion.

Pilate ordered a slave to fetch him a golden bowl with water. It was his last resort. Surely if he declared the execution of Yeshua a judicial murder, the crowd would respect this rarely used custom and let Yeshua go.

Pilate rose from the judgment seat to perform the symbolic act. He washed his hands in full view of the crowd.

"I am not guilty of this man's blood," he said. "You are the ones who are causing it."

Caiaphas led the crowd by calling out the Old Testament formula reply for accountability.

"We and our children will be responsible for his death!" Caiaphas shouted.

The frenzied crowd picked up the chant. "We and our children will be responsible for his death!"

Pilate spoke with weariness to a nearby guard. "Stauro-theto," he said, pronouncing his final verdict in Latin for the records.

Let him be crucified.

58

I remained on the edge of the cliff, uncaring of the passage of time.

I did not want to die, neither did I want to live.

What then, I asked myself again and again.

What then?

In a small courtyard surrounded by the soldiers' barracks, a centurion—his grizzled face reflecting his boredom with a duty he'd carried out dozens of times—organized the required soldiers and wood beams to execute the criminals sentenced earlier. A slave paced at the fringes of the group carrying two bags, one with nails and a hammer, the other with the provisions to last the soldiers during their guard vigils beneath the crosses.

Outside the barracks, in the early morning sunshine that already promised heat would later reflect from the city buildings, the narrow streets should have been quiet as the shops, bazaars, and markets had closed for a festival day. Yet a crowd of hundreds waited, lining both sides of the street into the quarter of Acra. Many in the crowd were the elders and Pharisees of the Sanhedrin, their gray beards bobbing as they discussed the events with great heat; Caiaphas and the chief priests had disappeared, choosing to present public disinterest once they had been assured of the death of the prophet. Many of the others, however, were friends of Yeshua and curious onlookers, astounded and helpless at hearing the man from Galilee had been captured and sentenced privately and quickly.

The centurion was finally satisfied that everything was ready. He carried a substantial paunch, his knees were arthritic, and he did not look forward to walking the steep cobblestone streets and beyond to the place of execution. So, with a long sigh and a tired wave of his hand, he sent the procession ahead to the street and the waiting spectators.

Their expectations of drama were not disappointed.

They saw a man with a crown of thorns pressed into his head, a man haggard from the pain of betrayal, whose mental anguish had been great enough to draw blood from the pores of his skin. He had not had food or drink during a sleepless night of inquisition, and his welted and bruised skin had been flayed raw the length of his body. He bent nearly double as he dragged the heavy beam of lumber that rested on his shoulders.

The crowd's first view of the fallen Messiah drew a ripple of gasps of excited horror.

Then the people closest to Yeshua read the inscription on a sign that dangled in Yeshua's face from the end of the beam, partially obscuring his vision. The gasps became exclamations of surprise, and the nearest elders quickly dispatched runners to Caiaphas.

Pilate had dispensed with the customary herald who carried a wooden board to proclaim the nature of the crime. Instead, he had ordered this sign, scrawled with a stick of gypsum, and written in Latin, Hebrew, and Greek so that no person would fail to understand the simple message:

Hail, the King of Jews!

Women on both sides of the street wept openly. Even had they not known the man or the situation, the pitiful sight would have torn their hearts.

Yeshua fell repeatedly beneath the weight of the beam. Where his body was not too badly ripped from his earlier whipping, his taut muscles lay flat against bone, showing a man accustomed to work and easily capable of such a load. But he had lost too much blood, suffered from physical shock, and reached the verge of unconsciousness from thirst. Because of the incline of the road and the uneven cobbles, he would have had difficulty simply walking without the burden of rough hewn lumber scraping against his raw back.

When he fell, the grizzled centurion dispassionately beat him with the side of his spear, as if Yeshua were a stubborn mule.

What tore most at the women's hearts was Yeshua's struggle to continue. He fell and bore the beatings silently, somehow getting to his feet one more time. Yet each time he stumbled, it took him longer to regain his feet, with effort so excruciatingly obvious that men in the crowd had to refrain from stepping forward to help him.

Some who read of my small part in this from other sources might say I was a traveler, just at that moment arriving in Jerusalem for the Passover. But what pilgrim would arrive *after* the Passover?

I had actually just slowly passed the villas and gardens of Bezetha, on my way back into Jerusalem. As I had my own share of misery—though none to compare with his—and as I was full of my own sorrow and emptiness, I did not see the procession until I was almost upon it, just outside the Tower Gate.

When I did lift my eyes, I merely saw a bloody man on his knees with a beam of lumber lying across the backs of his calves. A centurion repeatedly struck his shoulders with the side of his spear. The bloody man tried to push himself up, but simply collapsed again and again.

Behind him were two other men, also carrying cross beams. Each of the three was guarded by four soldiers.

Perhaps it was my sudden interest, or that the centurion faced my direction. Certainly it made a difference that I was a lone traveler heading into the city and easily noticed. Whatever the reason, the centurion's eyes met mine—and he beckoned me forward.

All eyes in the crowd turned on me.

"You," the centurion said to me. "Come here."

59

One did not ignore the command of Roman soldiers, so I obeyed. But not with fear. For one thing, I didn't care enough about my own life. For another, I knew I had the protection of money. Unless the centurion struck me dead on the spot, if he accused me of some offense—though I couldn't imagine what—I could easily hire a defense; Romans are sticklers for the law, and I believed I would not be unfairly tried.

"Carry this cross," the centurion said, tapping me on the shoulder with his spear to conscript me into service. "We go as far as the place of the skull."

Although I stood a head taller than the centurion, I obeyed without resistance. It would have been foolish to do otherwise.

Standing beside the man—who was still on his knees and gasping from exhaustion like a lathered, driven horse—I lifted the beam of wood and rested it on the meat of my right shoulder. He was so beaten, so bloody, that even then I paid no special attention to him. And, knowing how it felt to be utterly drained, I shifted my position and offered my free hand to help him up.

Not until he was on his feet, not until he lifted his face and shone those eternal eyes directly into my soul, did I recognize him.

Yeshua. The Messiah.

"Simon," he said, addressing me in the short form of my name. It came out as a mumbled whisper. His lips were swollen, and his tongue pushed against a snapped tooth. "Remember my instructions to you. And remember you are a child of God. Let him provide the healing."

Simon. The man knew my name!

Later, I would contemplate the compassion of a man who, in the depths of this degradation, reached out to me. Later, I would come to realize that he knows all of us by name. But then, in that moment, I could only marvel that he knew me.

Simon.

Before I could speak, women broke into weeping wails. They had taken advantage of the procession's halt and had moved to surround us. They threw themselves on the road in front of us, begging the centurion to set Yeshua free.

On his entrance into Jerusalem on the Sunday before, Yeshua had wept over the women of Jerusalem. Now, they wept for him.

Yeshua shook his head and spoke more clearly than I would have expected from a man so thoroughly beaten and exhausted.

"Women of Jerusalem, don't cry for me. Cry for yourselves and for your children. The time is coming when people will say, 'Happy are the women who cannot have children and who have no babies to nurse.' Then people will say to the mountains, 'Fall on us!' And they will say to the hills, 'Cover us!'"

They stared at him in amazement and bewildered disbelief. Infertility was a curse. She who did not bear her husband a child was looked down upon by all other women, in danger of being replaced by another wife. And, married or not, she faced poverty and lonely old age as a widow.

At that moment, with the weight of his cross firmly on my back, I shared their shock at his response to their crying out on his behalf.

In my old age, of course, I would understand the literal prophecy of his words. When the Romans laid siege on Jerusalem, stories reached me in Cyrene of desperate, frenzied women roasting and eating their own children. And, with the scattering of the Jews, there was good reason to fear what awaited our people in the centuries ahead.

Yet since that moment of straining to rise with his cross, I have also come to believe that Yeshua was firmly rejecting their pity—and mine—because it was misplaced. When all we see is the man, the fallen prophet, we fail to see his kingdom beyond. We mourn his suffering when, instead, we should mourn the reason he suffered—among the burdens he accepted by turning toward his place of execution were my own puny sins, my despair and hopelessness, and a selfishness that kept me apart from God.

I carried the cross for him.

Too soon, the hill of the skull loomed above us.

60

The messengers dispatched by Caiaphas reached Pilate, weary in his magistrate's chair.

By the way they were dressed, it was obvious who they were. And they could only be before him again for one reason. "Have I not finished your troublesome business?" Pilate asked.

"It is the sign on his cross," the first messenger said. "We have been instructed to tell you it should not be written 'The King of Jews' but 'This man said, "I am the King of the Jews."'"

Pilate leaned forward and glared, then he waved them away. "What I have written, I have written."

Golgotha, the hill of the skull, was just north of the city. It was not named, as many think, for skulls of the dead abandoned around the execution sites; Jewish law forbids exposure of human bones. Instead, as anyone can see, the hill of the skull is just that: a high, rounded rocky plateau like the dome of a man's head, worn by wind and rain to a dull gray. Two shallow caves, side by side, and a lower, larger cave centered below, form the eyes and gaping mouth. At certain times of day, when the sun's light casts black shadows across those depressions, it becomes such a vision of a gaunt face that any wind moaning across its barren stone seems to speak of the cries and groans and cursing of all the men who have died tortured deaths on the hill.

As we arrived, I heard new voices join the crowd, voices that began to stridently jeer Yeshua. It wasn't until the centurion allowed me to set down the beam of wood that I saw.

Caiaphas and the other priests had arrived, probably coming from temple services that allowed them, as always, to proclaim their holiness before God and man. They, and other elders, were circulating through the crowd, encouraging people to hurl insults at Yeshua as he stood bowed, waiting for the soldiers to begin the process of crucifixion.

Since Pilate had refused to alter the sign to read "This man said, 'I am the King of the Jews,'" it appeared the distinguished members of the Sanhedrin were now forced to participate in the crucifixion, if only to incite derision, fearing that some in the crowd might take the sign to heart.

If any other man had been standing there—beaten, nearly naked, crusted with blood, hands bound, and about to be nailed to a cross—their fear of him would have been ridiculous. But Yeshua, swaying as he was from hunger and pain, still commanded respect. He was like a large rock jutting high above the ocean, impervious to the loud, vain splashing of the waves against its base.

Behind him, into the ground, the soldiers planted the beam I had carried to this place of execution.

Crucifixion is a simple process. After the upright beam is positioned, the cross beam is set on the ground. The victim is forced onto his back and laid across it with his arms extended.

A long sharp nail is driven into each hand. Sometimes, when executioners have little skill or time, they pound the nail halfway up the flesh of the forearm, confident that eventually the victim's weight will tear the arm's soft flesh until the bones of the wrist meet the nails and arrest the downward slide of the body. Once the victim has been secured to the cross piece, soldiers use ropes to draw him upward, and bind the cross piece to the upright with rope or nails.

At this point, however, the soldiers are far from finished. If the victim were left hanging in this manner, death would arrive too quickly from suffocation as the body's unsupported weight pulled against the lungs.

So the soldiers turned the victim's lower body sideways and pushed the legs upward before driving spikes through the ankles.

Only then would the soldiers step aside.

The pain is so great that a man is sometimes unable to scream. His brain floods with agony from the different parts of his body. Flies arrive to settle on his blood and eyes and nose to torment him.

Yet the real pain has not yet begun.

He will usually choose the lesser agony of hanging from the nails in his hands, simply because it is unbearable to place any weight on the fragmented bones of his ankles. But he will begin to suffocate. His lungs will strain for the sweetness of air until his throat rattles.

A man's will to live is an unreasoning desperation, and it ignores his wish to die. So he fights for air by pushing up with cramping thigh muscles, supporting his weight on the iron spikes in his ankles.

When he can no longer endure this pain, he will sag again,

until his lungs suck for air and he pushes his weight on his ankles again. He will alternate between these two agonies, knowing it may take hours and sometimes days before exhaustion and dehydration finally send him into black oblivion.

And the entire time it takes to die, his body will only be a scant foot or two off the ground.

This death is what awaited Yeshua.

There is a merciful Jewish tradition that allows women to offer the condemned a cup of strong wine mixed with myrrh.

Yeshua refused it.

He said nothing as the soldiers drove him to his knees. Nothing as they pushed him onto his back. And nothing as the point of the first spike was pressed against his right palm.

As for me, I was a coward. I turned my head. The hammer came down with the peculiar clang and thud of iron hitting iron into wood. Against those two forces, iron's impact against the flesh is soundless, if not for the screams of the victim.

Yeshua, however, met the beginning of his death with full submission, as silent as a slaughtered Passover lamb before the altar.

When I found the courage to look again, blood streamed dark from his pierced palms and soaked into the hard, cold ground.

CYRENE

61

Upon my return to Cyrene, I did not disembark from the two-masted sailing vessel that had taken me the final leg of my journey from Alexandria. Instead, I remained aboard the ship in the harbor.

I had traveled for six weeks after leaving Jerusalem. During that time, I had spent hours deciding what I must do.

Even so, I had no certainty as to the right course of action.

I sent a messenger from the ship to Jaala, carrying the letters I had written during my Passover stay in Jerusalem. He also bore the scroll that would tell my wife the truth about the evening of the fire. . . .

As had been my custom, I had worked late into the afternoon at my accounts in the small warehouse, long after most men had returned to their homes and families. And, as had also been my custom, I had eased my solitude with wine. I was close to drunk as I worked through some difficult transactions in the light of an oil lamp.

I had forgotten. Jaala had planned a celebration to mark Vashti's birth date. My daughter arrived to tell me herself, her dark hair combed and pinned back, her dark eyes flashing with importance. She carried a kitten in her arms, one of many strays that tried my patience.

I became surly at Vashti's insistence to return home. When she reminded me of the celebration, my irritation increased, more at myself for having forgotten than at her.

Vashti set the kitten down on my table. She clutched at my hem as she begged me to set aside my work. The kitten stepped onto my accounts and I saw a place to vent my temper. I callously knocked the animal aside, and it tumbled into the oil lamp, beginning a horrible chain of events.

As the lamp fell, oil and fire spilled onto the fine wrap of silk around Vashti's legs. She shrieked in panic and pulled away from me before I could beat the flames into submission.

She ran; a growing flame snaked around her tender legs.

I stumbled after her.

In her desperation, she fell against an unsteady table, which crashed to the floor, pinning her in a pile of dry rags beneath the table. The flames took hold of the rags instantly, and her legs became a torch.

I tried to pull her away. I felt useless because of my wine-addled brain. In her terror, Vashti clawed at my face and arms. When I finally disentangled her from the table and rags, the fire had begun to spread.

I had to save Vashti before I could turn my efforts to stopping the fire. I flailed ineffectually at the flames on her legs. I finally realized I could snuff the fire by rolling my child in a rug. But by this time, too many valuable seconds had passed.

The fire around me had flickered from piles of cloth to piles of cloth. Stopping it was unlikely, obvious to me even in my impaired state. I picked Vashti up and, with her screams of agony in my ears, made an unsteady path of escape.

As smoke began to blind me, I fell twice. When I reached the air outside, I was grateful we were alive.

Vashti continued to scream. With a jolt, I became aware of a pattern in her screams and realized it was more than the crazed sounds of senseless desperation and pain. But I could not understand her hysterical words.

She tried to pull herself back into the warehouse and fought me as I restrained her.

By then, passersby had begun to run toward us, drawn by Vashti's shrieks. Others ran, shouting, to alert neighbors to the fire.

At some point in the confusion and screaming and roar of the growing fire, I noticed Jaala shaking my shoulder.

She had come to the warehouse because she could not find Ithnan. She had hoped to find our firstborn son—only six years old—with his older sister, for he followed Vashti everywhere.

And in that moment of horror, I understood Vashti's hysteria.

She'd brought him on her errand, knowing how he loved to explore the rolls of cloth and stacks of merchandise.

Ithnan was inside the burning warehouse.

I ran toward the great, roaring monster that held my firstborn son in its jaws.

Inside, I could see nothing. Just inside the door, swirling dense smoke drove me, choking, to my knees.

I yelled in desperation, crawling and sweeping with my hands, hoping to clutch the tiny ankles of my son.

A narrow beam of burning wood fell, striking me on the left side of my face, searing through my beard and skin. I didn't even feel the pain.

My son was somewhere in the fire. A fire of my doing.

Another beam struck my head. In my last moments of consciousness, I hoped for my own death.

I had fallen so near the entrance that those who fought the fire doused me and the flames with their first buckets of water. I was pulled from the wreckage of my business, close to death and hours from reviving, but alive.

Not so my firstborn son.

After the last of the fire had been tamed, someone discovered his body curled in a corner, spared from flame. But smoke had sucked the life from his lungs.

His body in death was as it had been in life. Perfect.

During the hours I had been unconscious, Vashti had shrieked over and over again that the fire had been her fault. In my first waking moments—unaware of Vashti's claim of responsibility and deeply ashamed—I had pretended confusion, determined to tell Jaala when the time was right.

Coward that I was, I delayed the truth again and again. The longer I let the lie continue and the more people heard it with grave sympathy, the more difficult it became to confess. Finally I could not turn back and take off the mantle of determined hero that had fallen upon me.

My torment had just begun.

My undivulged knowledge became a millstone of self-hatred, and as I closed myself off from Jaala, it destroyed what little love remained in our marriage.

Only a parent can truly comprehend the depths of my remorse, anguish, and self-loathing in the months that followed. Although I had not deliberately hurt my daughter, I was responsible. If, somehow, I could have blocked that responsibility from my mind and heart, her agony was there daily to remind me, not only in her cries of pain but also in the expression her eyes held and in how she recoiled from me when I tried to hug her.

I had burned her legs; I had seared her soul. I had once been her adored father, the man who could do anything and fix anything. Then in one horrible moment, I had betrayed her trust, destroyed her life, and killed my firstborn son.

Yet the world saw me as a valiant, heroic man for saving my daughter, for my struggle against the fire.

My remorse and anguish and self-loathing became the despair I had carried into Jerusalem.

62

As I waited on the ship during the first day in Cyrene, not ten minutes went by that I did not strain my eyes toward my villa on the nearby hillside.

My plea to Jaala had been simple. If she could take me back after hearing my letters and confession, she should hang a dark blanket from a window, easily visible to my hoping eyes.

I had intended to be noble and romantic in my efforts to win back her heart, refusing to shame her with my unworthy presence.

The hours of bright sunshine and blue sky passed to mock my despair. Instead of nobility, I was a fool. I had to restrain myself from rushing up the streets to beg at the door for a glimpse of her face.

The entire day passed.

As I waited, I tried to imagine her reaction. Had she heard the letters? The messenger had been greeted at the door by a servant, who would only confirm that the mistress of the household would accept them.

I tried to remain in seclusion on the ship; if Jaala would not have me back, I did not want to shame myself further by making her rejection public knowledge. Because of the seclusion, however, I did not dare make inquiries of my household. I did not even know if my daughter still lived.

Night fell. I settled into the bowels of the ship, hoping that every creak and every sway would signal Jaala stepping on board to throw herself into my arms. I did not sleep.

Dawn arrived. Jaala did not.

63

After another day, I could no longer fool myself. Enough time had passed. Jaala had made her decision. I could wait years and the blanket would not appear at a window of our villa.

Still, I did not order the boat to set sail.

This near, I could not leave. I imagined Jaala's every move in the villa. In my mind, I listened as she hummed, watched as she brushed her hair, stood beside her as she looked down on my ship in the harbor.

All the while, I knew a final goodbye was approaching. Once the ship left the harbor, I would not return. I planned to revisit Jerusalem. I could manage my business affairs from there and see to it that Jaala lived a good life without me. It would not be a hopeless existence for me. Keen as I would miss her, despair no longer overwhelmed my soul. Pascal would welcome me in Jerusalem, as would some of the followers of Yeshua, for I had turned to them in the days after the crucifixion, seeking answers about the man on the cross and the final events of that Friday. . . .

I remained at the cross as the soldiers gambled for the rights to keep Yeshua's seamless clothing. I remained in the afternoon as a darkness covered the land—caused, perhaps, by a rare but not unheard of dust storm swirling above us or by an event astronomers could have predicted from the way stars moved in the sky. I remained until Yeshua cried out that it was finished, as the roar of an earthquake punctuated his last words, as the centurion was forced to exclaim that surely the man on the cross was the Son of God. I watched the soldiers thrust a spear into Yeshua's motionless body to make sure he was dead. I saw watery blood spill from the hole in his side. I was there when the soldiers broke the legs of the two thieves to hasten their death before sundown, still there as the thieves rattled their last breaths, suffocating because their legs supported them no longer.

When Yeshua's body was taken from the cross, I finally returned to Pascal and Seraphine. Pascal had found my note to him along with the document and the sealed letters. He gave them all back to me without asking why I had intended to take my life, and without asking why I had changed my mind. He was a good friend.

After, I searched out as many followers as I could, asking questions about the man of miracles; my brief contact with him compelled me to learn about him.

Judas, I discovered, had died hours before the man he had betrayed. After hearing the verdict against Yeshua, he had flung the silver back at the high priests, and remorse drove him to the act I could not do. He was discovered days later hanging from a branch by the same girdle he'd once used to store his thirty pieces of silver.

I am convinced, however, that Yeshua would have forgiven Judas. For I had watched as Yeshua died in agony on the cross, yet he was concerned not about himself, but others. To the thief beside him, Yeshua had promised that heaven waited. Upon seeing his mother weeping, Yeshua had pledged her into a disciple's care. For the jeering crowd, he had prayed that God forgive them.

Many times I have wondered about this request. What I have decided is this: Yeshua had a heart that saw much more than any other man. On the cross, looking down at the crowd, he felt and understood the pain and the burdens each person carried. A Pharisee, perhaps, had worries about a son who preferred wine and harlots to religious instruction. Maybe a woman was racked with the grief of losing a child. Or another man sleepless with the agony that accompanies doubts about a wife's faithfulness. Each of them—as with all of us—would have kept those fears private, unknown to the rest of the world. Each of them—as with all of us—had the heartache, hurts, and sorrows that come with lives lived apart from God.

As Yeshua saw their pain, he saw, too, that most of the people in the crowd were so intent on their own lives, so apart from God's presence that they failed even to look to God for help. He saw them as the poor, pitiable, weak creatures that they were.

Yet he knew what would heal them and give them peace: God's love, given freely. And so the plea from the man condemned to die because of his love for those in need: *Father, forgive them, because they don't know what they are doing.*

This is why I believe Yeshua would have embraced Judas, had Judas truly wished it.

All of this, I believe to be true, even if Yeshua was only man.

But if he was only man, his forgiveness would not have erased my guilt as it did.

As I learned more about Yeshua and what he did and taught, I began to understand he was the Passover lamb who had stood in my place. This lamb, unlike any other lamb, had gone to his death willingly and aware. No other altar sacrifice was needed for me to be able to approach God, to have the mask of my selfishness removed so that I could see the warmth of the light that had always been there.

If Yeshua was only man, I would not have found the joy in the peace that had sent me home to Cyrene with hope. . . .

When, finally, I gave reluctant orders for the ship to prepare to sail, I remained on deck, staring at the white of my villa so hard and long that my eyes ached from the brightness of the sun.

I still wanted to believe Jaala would take me back. Perhaps the activity on the ship—if she were watching—would show her I would act upon my word. Perhaps, with my departure looming, she would have a change of heart.

In those minutes before departure, I resigned myself to life without her. But I was not without a certain joy. In Jerusalem, I had found a redemption. I knew I could begin to live life looking forward, not back.

As two of the crew began to untie the heavy ropes that held the ship to the wharf, I heard a cry that was almost lost among the shrieking of the gulls overhead.

I saw a girl, running toward the ship.

Vashti? Yes! Unless my eyes and my hope had deceived me.

I stopped the men and jumped from the ship.

The child continued to run toward me.

My daughter was running!

Her face was bright with joy as she jumped into my arms.

Her body felt to tiny and vulnerable that it almost broke my heart to think I had to leave.

I set her down and squatted so I could look into her beautiful face.

"Mama wanted you to see that I can walk," she said proudly. "My legs are not pretty, but they don't hurt and I can walk and run."

I spoke slowly, afraid my voice would break and alarm her.

"I am so very glad," I said. For the healing. And that Jaala had sent her. As a gift, it would console me over the lonely years ahead. That the scars remained would always remind me of my own journey from desperation to healing.

"Ithnan is happy too," she said. "He told me it was what he wanted."

Before I could express surprise or disbelief, she quickly explained, as if she had done so many times with many other adults.

"It was in a dream," she said. "Ithnan talked to me in a dream."

Not once in the eighteen months after the fire had Vashti been able to even hear his name without becoming hysterical.

"Tell me about your dream," I said softly.

Her eyelids dropped.

"It's important to me," I said.

She began shyly. "I felt silver light that was like a bright star alone in a dark sky. It turned brighter and warm until it filled the sky. It was Ithnan's home. He spoke from the light. He told me he liked it there and that I should not feel bad for him. He told me he wanted me to walk. When I woke up in the morning, I was happier and my legs started to get better."

"Was that yesterday?" I asked, teasing her with a smile. I was ready to believe her if she said yes.

"No, Papa. Since Passover."

Since Passover. Miracle or coincidence? Some, I am sure, will say that deep in her mind, my little girl needed to overcome her own guilt before allowing herself to heal. Some will say that the act of the Passover sacrifice sparked some form of self-forgiveness inside her. Some will say that she healed in the weeks since Passover as part of a natural process.

I knew what I believed, however, and I closed my eyes in a prayer of gratitude.

When I opened my eyes, she was looking at me gravely. With innocence. God must be thanked that our children love us without condition, that Vashti was too young to see me as the driven man who had disappointed her mother so badly. God must be thanked that the scars on her soul had begun to heal.

"Will you tell Mama that I love her very much?" I asked. "If she changes her mind, she can send word to Jerusalem. I will be there . . ."

I lost my voice. It took several seconds to compose myself. "I will be there because of work."

An easy escape to give Vashti. She'd heard it often enough before.

"Don't you want to tell her yourself?" Vashti asked. She took my hand. "Mama sent me running down here to reach you before your ship left. She wants you to come home."

Epilogue

Away from the weeping chamber of my own tomb, I now sit in the shade of my villa. I occasionally stir, moving into the sun like a wrinkled lizard, warming the loose, leathered skin that wraps my old bones. Beyond my courtyard are the masts of ships in the harbor. The breathtaking blue expanse of the Mediterranean spreads beyond to meet a cloudless azure sky.

Forty years have passed since my firstborn son died. My thoughts return to the weeping chamber where I stood so recently to mourn him. I am saddened as much by my memories of him as by the knowledge that too soon I will return to the weeping chamber.

And forty years after the events of that Friday, I am able to see more clearly why an innocent man died.

The crowd before Pilate had no notion how prophetic their call for Yeshua's blood to be upon them and their children would be. Word has recently reached me that Jerusalem has fallen. After a six-month siege, the Romans—efficient, determined, ruthless—ended what was at the beginning plainly inevitable to all but the foolish rebel Jews who expected God to rescue them as he had patiently aided Moses, Joshua, David, and all the other heroes whom descending generations of Jews so proudly wear as cloaks of armor. Yet, despite the self-righteous, unceasing, directive prayers that surely rose from Jerusalem, no sea was parted, no pestilence destroyed the enemy, no trumpet calls brought them down, no angel of death visited the Roman army camps. Instead, the mighty city walls were finally broken, the Jewish rebels crucified, and, in the haze of the fire of destruction that drifted across the city, with the background yells of soldiers joyfully pursuing women in the rubble of torn streets, the temple stones were pushed off the plateau to tumble onto the tombs below.

Jerusalem—as Yeshua had predicted—is no more.

Some might say it is fanciful to assert that Jerusalem fell because a small minority of Jews slaughtered an innocent man, but I believe there is some truth in the statement.

Rome would have been content to coexist with Jerusalem for centuries—the mighty empire only fights back when prodded. Jerusalem fell because in the end Rome could no longer tolerate the unchanged religious blind selfishness, hypocrisy, and fanaticism that had killed Yeshua those four decades earlier.

Jerusalem is no more.

I am grateful that Pascal and Seraphine did not behold the siege. Pascal died gently in his sleep a dozen years ago, and the rich widow Seraphine married a silk trader in Alexandria.

Pilate is gone, recalled to Rome a few years after Yeshua's crucifixion for putting down a Samaritan riot with too much force. Some rumors have it that he killed himself as his career faded. Others that his wife Procula became a follower and led Pilate to the same hope and belief in a man he had ordered crucified.

Peter is gone, too, martyred on a cross for refusing to deny Yeshua one more time. He declined the honor of dying the same way as his beloved master, however, and the executioners granted his request to be crucified upside-down.

I do not know the fate of Caiaphas. Violent or peaceful, whatever end Caiaphas reached is one he deserved. Hatred is its own punishment. The riches his schemes continued to accumulate would not have been worth the last moments of consciousness and the sudden awareness of how utterly cold and lonely it will be for his soul's travel beyond.

My servant has appeared on the villa balcony to interrupt my thoughts. His hands are empty of the cooled juice I had expected. Instead, he has brought a message.

"She calls for you."

I don't ask why. The expression on my servant's face tells me enough.

Slowly, I push myself to my feet. I lean on his arm as he takes me inside.

We enter a room in the upper corner, then the servant departs.

I smile at Vashti, who sits beside the bed where she has spent many hours away from her husband and family over the past weeks. Her face is barely composed. While I see in her grief the young girl who clung to me during the sorrows of her innocence, I also see strength and dark-haired beauty, much like Jaala's face in our early years together.

Vashti's younger brothers, our sons Alexander and Rufus whom Jaala bore in the happier days that followed my return, would be here, too, but they are helping to establish the Word in other parts of the empire. It is impossible for them to return in time.

Vashti rises and steps away from the bed, allowing me to move close.

It is hot, but the woman I love shivers beneath her blankets. Jaala. My wife. God's gift to me. Twice.

My chest is tight with grief. I go to her, blinking away tears.

Although, like me, she is old, and others might see wrinkles in her face, I only see the beauty that entranced me during the songs she softly sang throughout the years. Her body has become so tiny. Her once-dark hair is as white as mine. The delightful strong hands that stroked my face in our youth are now withered, knotted into fists as she fights occasional spasms of pain.

I sit beside her and take one of her hands. I brush her knuckles against my cheek. I do not trust my voice enough to speak first.

"I love you," she says when she finds the energy.

"As I do you."

A part of my mind notices that Vashti has left the room to give us privacy.

When, long ago in the temple, I begged Yeshua to heal Vashti, I had not understand his reply. I had yet to realize that forgiveness earned or bought is not forgiveness, but a transaction. Forgiveness must be given by the one who has been wronged, accepted as a gift by the one who has done the wrong.

When a wrong cannot be righted, men have the power to punish.

But who has the power to forgive?

The sun is lower now, and shadows creep longer on the walls as I sit with Jaala, stroking her hair while she lays still with her eyes closed. I cannot imagine my life without her presence, yet the unimaginable is approaching as surely as the sun must disappear with the shadows that darken.

Jaala opens her eyes.

She sees that I am weeping.

Tears form in her eyes too.

With so many memories and so much I still want to say, I find I can only fall back on what means the most to me on earth.

"I love you," I say.

"And I you," she says. But her smile is small and her voice a whisper. We both know it will not be long.

Her eyes flutter and close.

As she fades from me, I can hardly bear my grief. To console myself, I remind myself I have something to grieve, when I once thought she was gone from me forever.

I received forgiveness through Yeshua. It brought me home. But his forgiveness is worthless if he is only man, not Messiah. He cannot be accepted halfway. If the miracles did not truly happen as miracles, he died justly—insane, a fraud, a blasphemer.

How does one decide? Other men in the temple saw cripples walk at his touch, yet in their disbelief they looked for other explanations. Thus, it makes no difference whether a man witnesses miracles with his own eyes or hears of them later—even centuries later—from those who were there.

It is, of course, a matter of faith. But faith has two edges; some use determined disbelief to transform miracles into something natural, while others too eagerly transform natural wonders into miracles.

And so truth becomes lost in the confusion.

Jaala wakes and squeezes my hand, this beautiful woman who pledged her life to me.

There is sweat on her forehead. With a damp cloth, I soothe her heated skin.

Her eyes close again. I cannot help myself. I lean down and lightly touch my lips to hers, knowing all the tender kisses we shared will too soon be only memories.

Her eyes remain closed as she whispers her last request. "Sing to me, my love."

I am not sure I understand her words, such is her weakness.

"Sing to me, my love," she whispers again.

And so I sing to her. It is the first time. Always, in our many years together, she has sung to me.

We each have a soul that continues beyond the body. This I know. During our lives on earth, we hide ourselves from the One who created our souls—our self-absorption and our vain pursuits of the flesh become a chasm that prevents us from full awareness of him. None of us can cross that chasm without acknowledging he is there and waiting, without asking for a bridge to reach him.

That bridge is Yeshua—but only if we believe he is who he claimed to be.

I am still quietly singing when life leaves Jaala.

I only know she is gone because her hand relaxes in mine.

I continue to sing because I am determined not to let myself know she has died. As long as I sing, I tell myself, she is still listening to me.

But I am old. My voice begins to fail me.

When I can sing no longer, I place my head on her chest and let my tears soak into the blanket that covers her.

I was not there after the crucifixion when Joseph of Arimathea went to Pilate for permission to bury Yeshua in a private tomb. Nor when the Pharisees requested and received from Pilate continuous armed guard at the entrance of the tomb, worrying that Yeshua's followers might steal away the body—who had been proven dead with the spear thrust in his side—and proclaim that the Messiah rose from the dead as he had promised. Nor was I there when another earthquake struck Jerusalem early on Sunday morning, scattering the guards and opening the sealed tomb.

I was, however, in the tomb later that Sunday, to look myself after the rumors began that Yeshua was alive.

I had to stoop to enter the tomb. When I straightened, I stood in the weeping chamber, the very place where tears had anointed his still, pierced body as faithful followers had wrapped him in linens and spices three days earlier.

I looked at his burial place and saw all that remained were the empty burial linens.

A smile crossed my face as I noticed the wrap that had been used to cover Yeshua's face. The cloth had been folded in half, then folded in half once again and left neatly on the stone floor beside the burial linens.

Standing in that weeping chamber, years after Yeshua had set aside his carpenter tools, I understood. And I began to feel an unfamiliar emotion. Joy.

The folded cloth was a simple method, traditional among carpenters, for most could not write. At the completion of a project, a carpenter took water from a bowl to wash the sawdust off his arms and face, dried himself, and folded the towel in the same way, leaving it behind so anyone arriving later would understood the same message Yeshua had left for us in the empty tomb on that Sunday:

It is finished.

No one disturbs my grief.

My wife's hand is now cold. Since the fall of night, I have not moved from her bedside, nor have I let go of her hand.

Dawn has begun the new day. A day without Jaala.

But I am not without hope.

I believe.